good

Copyright © 2021 by Rae B. Lake

All rights reserved.

No part of this book may be reproduced in any form or by any electronic or mechanical means, including information storage and retrieval systems, without written permission from the author, except for the use of brief quotations in a book review.

JOSIP'S SECRET

JURIC CRIME FAMILY
BOOK TWO

RAE B. LAKE

ACKNOWLEDGMENTS

To My Not so secret lover- How many times have I asked you a question about a certain tool or electrical device. I'm so happy that now instead of actually thinking I need to fix something, you know that I'm going to use it in one of my books to do something sinister to one of my characters. It's so awesome that you never judge me for it either…lol.

To my guarded queens- I hope you know that you never have to be ashamed of who you are and who you love. No matter what, momma will love you forever.

To my friends, family and readers- I really love how Josip will go through anything to get the woman he loves. Nothing should ever come between two people who love each other. I hope you enjoy the story!

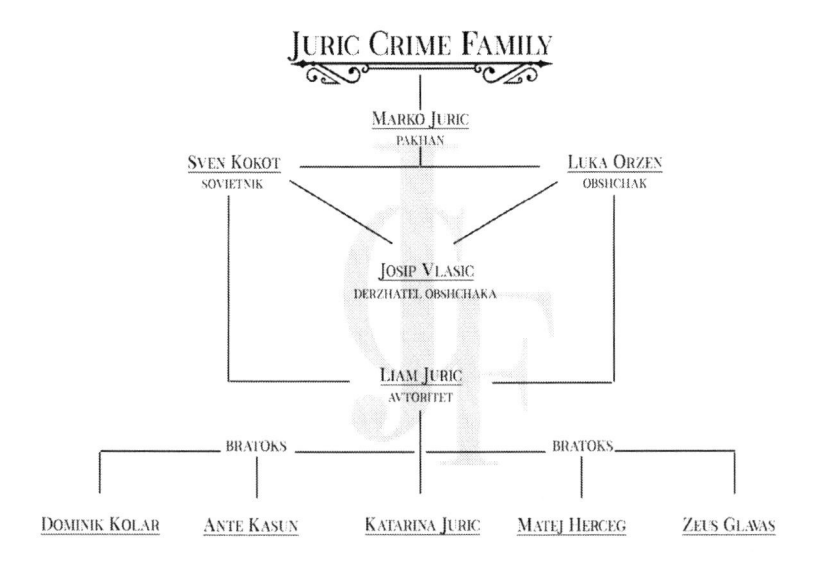

JURIC CRIME FAMILY

MARKO JURIC
PAKHAN

SVEN KOKOT
SOVIETNIK

LUKA ORZEN
OBSHCHAK

JOSIP VLASIC
DERZHATEL OBSHCHAKA

LIAM JURIC
AVTORITET

— BRATOKS —   — BRATOKS —

DOMINIK KOLAR   **ANTE KASUN**   **KATARINA JURIC**   **MATEJ HERCEG**   **ZEUS GLAVAS**

Allied Families
VAVRA CRIME FAMILY, DELUCA CLAN, SEVER CRIME FAMILY

DISCLAIMER

This book includes several graphic traumatic events that may be troubling/triggering for some readers. Discretion is advised.

1

JF

Josip

"What the hell do you mean they were attacked? How in the fuck does something like that happen? Luka this is on you. You were supposed to make sure this shit didn't happen!" Sven is in rare form today. Usually, you can count on him to keep his cool, but when it comes to the family business, he takes shit very hard.

"Jebote, don't you think I know that shit Sven. You think I'm just sitting on my ass as this shit is going down? Whoever it is has been hitting us at the most perfect times like they know everything about what we do. I'm only one fucking person." Luka's chest rises and falls as he heaves out his breath.

"Fine. Josip, what have you heard about what's going on?"

They both turn to me, expecting me to have the answers that both of them are desperate to find and Marko Juric is impatiently waiting for.

"I can't be certain as to who is pulling the strings, but all the hits that have happened in the last month seem to be linked to the Sever family."

"Then what the hell are we still sitting here for if we know it's them. Let's go over there and rip their fucking heads off." Luka jumps out of his chair, ready to go to war with the leader of one of our newest and shakiest of allies.

"Impossible, Ivan knows better." Sven isn't as quick to pull the trigger on that. He is married to Ema, and Ivan is her uncle. She doesn't care for the man, but if we were about to go to war with the Severs then she couldn't be trusted. I'm sure Sven wouldn't be looking forward to that. I happen to agree with Sven, we have quite a few deals in the making with the Sever family, it doesn't make sense for them to be robbing us in transit. Half of the merchandise that the thieves are taking from us is theirs and they would get no reimbursement.

"As much as I would love to sit here and debate with the two of you this is above my pay grade. I will be meeting with Matej and would prefer to make it there on time." I press the lock on my iPad and pack it away in my briefcase.

Technology is a double-edged sword. On one hand, I could take all the paperwork I would ever need around with me. On the other, if I ever lost this iPad and someone were able to break the encryption, I would be up shit creek.

This is a fucked-up situation to be in, but honestly, it's not my concern. I'm the bookkeeper. I take the notes and make sure people hold up to their agreements, nothing less. If there were a problem with that then Luka or Sven would have them taken care of. As the Drezhatel Obshchaka, I answer to only the two of them and Marko himself. I don't think I have ever had to lift an aggressive finger in all the time that I have been working for Marko Juric.

My worth lies in what I know. Because of that, I could get away with not getting my hands dirty.

"Yeah, I want to know everything he knew about the shit that was going on over there in Ireland. I worry Yemen might try to blow the whistle while he is locked up." Sven rubs a hand across the back of his neck.

"I doubt that, he's gained a whole new slew of clients while locked up. If he snitches, he'll lose a lot of money." I shrug and make my way to the door.

"Shit, are you serious?" Luka looks to me. "How the hell do you know that?"

I chuckle and walk out the door. There's no reason for me to answer him. I know about that the same way I know about him owing Ilia Vavra two million dollars. The same way I know that Sven has bought out two crabbing boats for Ema's father. Anytime money changes hands or there is a deal brokered, I'm the one making sure that everything is legit.

The guards that are standing by the door to make sure that we are not interrupted part ways. Luka's home is nowhere near as large as Marko's, but I would have to say it is the most ostentatious. The walls are decorated with golden wallpaper and a large crystal chandelier that stretches from the entrance all the way though the main foyer. The dual staircase is lined with a plush red carpet. Even his chairs were made for a king.

One of the guards steps forward and speaks to me directly, "Mr. Vlasic, there was a call from Liam Juric. He asked that you reach out to him at your earliest convenience."

"I see, thank you."

Fuck, there is no reason for him to be calling me. If he were calling for me then something must be going on with the bratoks.

I walk out the main entrance and down the steps stopping right in front of one of Luka's sports cars. There are three in the driveway alone.

I take out my phone and call Liam.

"Josip."

"Da?"

"I know it's last minute, but I need you to sit in on a meeting with some of the De Luca family. With Yemen going to jail they want to make sure that we are still on the same page."

"Of course, will they be joining us here or do we need to take a flight?" Nerves begin to explode in my gut.

"I'm thinking a flight would smooth things over a bit. No one expected Yemen to fuck this up so royally and now we are all trying to cover our losses." Liam sighs, his agitation palpable even through the phone.

"I'll pack a bag and meet you at the airstrip tomorrow morning. Send over the flight information." I hang up the phone before he can say anything else. There's no need for any other pleasantries.

A small smile spreads on my face. I don't care that I have to make a last-minute trip, and it's not like I like the De Lucas any more than any other family we are allied with, but I know that with this trip I'll be able to see Bella.

Orabella De Luca is the illegitimate child of Andrea De Luca. She is completely untouchable and I'm in love with her.

2

Josip

2 years earlier

"I'd like to raise a toast to our dear friends. It's not very often that we get to spend time with each other just to find out how the other is living. It's been too long since we've had a meeting like this one." Andrea De Luca stands from his seat and raises his glass. Everyone around him does the same. There is a round of cheers and clinking of glasses. I make sure to follow suit. The last thing I want is to be seen as disrespectful. Luka and Sven are walking around with Marko. Shaking hands and smiling at the same people that would have no trouble killing each and every one of us if the need were to arise.

The truce with the De Luca clan is long standing and for the most part, all of our joint ventures have always come up incredibly profitable. It's only recently that both sides have been organizing this social dinner. I think that it's just more of the De Lucas checking up on us, but that is nothing out of the norm. Everyone always wants to make sure that their allies are strong and if not, we are expendable.

Marko Juric is the most powerful leader out of all the different families of the Croatian Mob. I have no doubt that the De Lucas are going to want to keep us around for as long as they can.

"You don't seem to be having a lick of fun here." A woman with a tray says as she saunters in my direction.

"Pardon me?"

"You look bored."

"Ah, well, I'm not of much use at these sorts of things. I'm usually only called on when there is business to be done. The handshaking, I leave for Sven and Luka." I gesture towards the two of them with my chin.

"That's too bad. I would love to see more of you at these events." The woman rubs herself close to me and I grab her hand before she can complete her task. Her pointer and middle fingers inside my jacket pocket trying to lift whatever valuables she found there.

"You know I could have you killed for even attempting to steal anything from me." I growl low at her and watch as her face crumbles in fear. Her eyes tear up and I can see her pulse begin to race on the side of her neck. She is scared and she has every reason to be. Who the fuck tries to steal something in a room full of killers? I commend her bravery, but her stupidity is off the charts.

"Please, I ... I didn't ..."

I let go of her arm and wave my hand in her direction before she can even think about trying to get me to believe whatever excuse she is trying to come up with. "If I hear of any one of my people missing anything, I'll make sure that they know it was you. I promise that isn't how you want to die. My family is ruthless and they will take no pity on the fact that you're a woman." I stare her down for a second and wait for her to nod her understanding. She does and quickly moves away from me.

I toss down the last of my drink and walk out of the large area. I could have brought attention to the fact that there is someone walking around probably stealing wallets, but honestly, I don't want to go through the hassle. If she is dumb enough to try that shit with anyone else in the room, then she deserves the death she is bound to receive. I, on the other hand, just wanted to get out of here. We would be the De Lucas' guests for another three days. I'm sure they would see enough of me tomorrow and wouldn't miss me tonight.

The De Luca family has a large home near Fort Worth, with more than enough space to have all of us stay comfortably but it feels like a coffin in there.

I walk around the building searching for a place to get away from everyone. There is a small garden with a plethora of blooming flowers, ornately trimmed hedges, and a few benches. It seems like the perfect place for me to just hide out. I find a spot and try to relax. I let my head fallback and stare up at the stars, it's been a while since I've been able to see them so clearly. Sure, Las Vegas had the same sky, but something about the smog or the bright lights from the strip seemed to dull the bright lights up above. This same sky is far less sensational back home.

A soft scuffling sound grabs my attention. I don't speak a word. A tall woman gracefully walks into the same space that I'm in. For the first time in my life, I can say that someone has successfully taken my breath away. She has long brown hair that is slightly curled at the ends. She's thin and though I can only see the profile of her face, I can make out the slightly upturned slope of her nose and the plumpness of her lips. She walks directly into my line of sight, but doesn't realize that I'm sitting right there in front of her. Her eyes focus on the stone beneath her feet until she gets to a bunch of flowers. She bends slightly and smells them. If I'm not mistaken, I would say that they are lilies. The woman leans her head to the side and I watch as her eyes flutter shut. Suddenly the urge to smell whatever could have put that blissful look on her face overtakes my senses.

"Must smell wonderful." The tone of my voice is deep as I keep my eyes trained on her face.

"Oh God!" Her eyes pop open and she turns toward me. Her eyes sweep the area back and forth a few seconds and I realize that she mustn't be able to see me. I was wearing all black and sitting in a shadowy area, but I shouldn't have been that hard to make out. "Who's there?" she asks with a tremble to her voice.

I stand up and move further into the light. "I apologize, I didn't mean to startle you."

She just nods once, "Who are you?"

"Josip Vlasic, I'm a guest of Mr. De Luca." I reply and take a step in her direction. When she shies back, I realize she must see me as a threat.

"I'm sorry, I didn't realize there was anyone else here. Usually, there never is. I'll be on my way." She turns and tries to leave the small garden.

"Hey, wait a minute. I didn't mean to run you off. I'll just go back to my bench if you wish. You just looked so happy to be smelling that flower that I found myself a bit envious." I back up towards the bench and wait for her to make a decision as to whether or not she would stay. I came out here for solidarity, but now I find myself hoping that she will stay.

"Really, you don't mind me being out here with you?" She steps closer.

"No, why would I?"

"Hmm, you don't know who I am?"

"No. Should I?" The wheels in my head begin to turn as I try to place her face. I come up blank. I was better with numbers, faces not so much. And hers is a face I am sure I would remember. Now that she is facing me, I can see just how beautiful she truly is. Her eyes are almost a clear blue and her lips are bright pink. She has a small beauty mark right on the apple of her left cheek and even in the dim light I can see her eyelashes brushing against the top of her cheeks.

"No, I'm no one important."

"I highly doubt that." I let my eyes roll down her body and the loose dress that she is wearing. "Do you want to sit with me for a while?"

"Can you come further into the light?"

I take a few steps forward and a pleasant smile crosses her face. "Is this better?"

"Yes, sorry about that. I have nyctalopia, night blindness. It's mild, but I still have a bit of a hard time."

Now it makes sense why she couldn't find me earlier. "Ah, I see." I take another step in her direction, "Hopefully this makes it a bit easier?"

"Yes, thank you." She wrings her hands together before she drops them down by her side. "If you are a guest of Mr. De Luca than why are you out here? Shouldn't you be inside enjoying the party?"

"They would probably want me to, but if I'm going

to be honest with you, I'm not really into big crowds or for acting like I want to be somewhere when I really don't. No, I think me being able to get away for a little while is best for everyone." I take a step back, "Would you like to sit?" I motion to the bench. This time she nods her head.

"It sounds like you're missing a hell of a party in there Mr. Vlasic." She sits down with all the grace of a swan.

"I like the view better out here." I smirk at her and watch as her face drops down and a crimson color paints her pale cheeks. "What is your name?"

"Bella."

"It's very nice to meet you, Bella." I put my hand out for her to shake and she grabs hold. Desire shoots through my fingers and ricochets around my body like an errant bullet.

"You as well." I let go of her hand and sit back on the bench. "I haven't seen you all night. Have you been hiding away here in the garden?"

"No, I've been upstairs mostly. I'm not really invited to events like these which is perfectly fine for me." She sits back and absentmindedly fiddles with the fabric of her dress.

"A shame. The dinner was quite remarkable."

"Oh, what was served?" She turns toward me, the image of her crystal-clear blue eyes sears into my mind.

"A roast lamb."

"Yes, Ana's lamb is very good. I'm sure there will be more later." She smiles and I find myself leaning closer to her, completely enthralled by the words coming out of her mouth.

For the next few hours, we engage in easy conversation—from the food to the location, to some of her favorite pastimes. It's the most at ease I've felt in a long while. We move from the bench to walk around the garden and just enjoy each other's company.

"Trust me if you like stories like that then Red Rising is definitely a book you should read." She chuckles and swerves into my path slightly. I grab her waist to keep from bumping into her, but that one moment of contact is enough to light the air around us on fire. I hold onto her and stand right in front of her. I feel her stiffen and her eyes go wide as I get closer into her space.

"Bella, are you marked? Intended for someone? Anything like that?" At this moment all I want to do is kiss her, but I know if she does belong to someone else it may be enough to cause a falling out between the De Lucas and the Juric Family. I would never want to be the cause of that.

"Hmm ... No. Nothing like that." Her voice is soft and her gaze flickers back and forth between my lips and my eyes.

"Thank God." This is all I need. I hope she feels the same draw to me as I feel for her. I've known her for only a few hours and already I know that this woman is about to change my life. Everything inside of me wants to just slam my mouth to hers. I want to lift her off her feet, hike that dress up, and bury myself deep within her. Only as I lean forward to take her lips, the most fragile sound I've ever heard slips past her lips. This isn't the time to ravage her like I want, no this is the time for tenderness. I want to taste every part of her. To truly experience every swipe of her tongue and every crease on her lips.

I press my mouth to hers softly and she slowly pushes her trembling hands up my chest and clasps them behind my neck. I grab hold of her waist tighter and pull her closer to me. I want there to be no space between us. Her hands find their way into my hair and she tugs softly. I'm not going to be able to keep things soft and gentle for too much longer. I was in a relationship recently and my ex comes back from time to time solely to have sex. I'm not desperate for carnal attention, but something about Bella has me feeling like a teenage boy.

"Can we go back inside?" I pull away from her and mutter against her lips.

"Josip, I ..." She moans slightly and moves back in to kiss me more. The kisses are becoming more urgent and she is grinding herself into me as we continue to make out in a way that I've not done in years.

"Bella." I groan out just as she swerves her hips against my hard cock.

She pulls back almost startled, "Oh, I'm so sorry. We can't do this. I shouldn't have ..." She pushes her hands into her hair and takes a few steps back.

"What? What's the matter? I thought you said that you weren't attached to anyone."

"I'm not, but I still can't do this. I shouldn't have done this."

I take another step in her direction and she steps back. "Bella, I don't understand."

"I'm sorry, I'm so sorry. I had a great time. I'm sorry. I have to go." She shoots me a pitiful look before she literally turns and runs off.

"Bella!" I scream after her, my mind is going in a million directions trying to figure out what I might have done to freak her out so badly. I watch her long hair fly behind her as she runs out of the garden leaving me there confused and utterly entranced. One thing I know for sure is this won't be the last time I will be seeing her.

3

Josip

The next morning, I wake up and instead of worrying about the agenda for the day I'm more concerned with trying to find out where Bella is. I don't want to ask any of the people that work for the De Lucas in fear that she will get in trouble, but I don't think I can go through the entire day without seeing her.

I go to the one man that usually has all the answers—Sven.

He is already sitting down for his coffee and eggs when I walk into the dining room that the De Lucas set up for us to use.

"Dobro Jutro." I pull up a seat on the opposite side of the table and one of the workers comes out with a cup and a pitcher of coffee. I look up at her and give her my thanks.

"You're up early." I look in Sven's direction. I need to figure out a way to broach the subject without making it look as if I'm searching for her because of something that she's done.

"I'm always up early. What do you need Josip?" Sven puts his cup down and folds his hands on the table. Straight to the point, I should know by now that I can't beat around the bush when it comes to him. Sven is a no-nonsense man. He rarely has time for small talk.

"Are you aware of any of the workers with the name of Bella here? Maybe a grounds keeper or maid? Anything like that?"

"No, is there a problem? I'm sure that Leo and his father will want to know about anything like that."

"No, nothing like that. I was just curious. I ran into her last night, but wasn't able to get any information as to what she did here on the grounds." I shrug my shoulder and take another sip of coffee, making sure to keep my eyes locked on his.

A small smile hitches up one side of Sven's face. "I see, well Josip, I know that you are the epitome of discretion, but I should warn you that getting involved with anyone here may not end well. As far as I know, everyone is pretty much spoken for. I'd leave this one alone if I were you."

"Of course, it was just idle curiosity." I give him a tight nod before I stand up, leaving him at the table alone. I don't need Sven to tell me what I already know. The only hope I have is that she isn't part of the family. If she is just a worker, maybe the De Lucas won't mind so much if I pursue her.

I have to find a way.

* * *

"Your town is beautiful, truly." I tell Christian who has been charged by Leo to take Sven, Luka, and I out to see the sights. I've been to Texas many times before, but I'm not going to spit on their hospitality. Besides, if Mr. Juric needs me, he will let me know before I leave.

After breakfast I spend a little time searching for Bella, but I have no luck. After a while, I start to really think about what Sven said. Whatever it is that I'm feeling or thinking about will never work. Bella lives here with the De Lucas and I live in Vegas working for the Juric family. There is nothing more than a quick fuck that could come from this.

"I'm glad you enjoyed yourself. There will be drinks and cigars if you want to join us." Christian walks toward the front of the house, leaving the three of us by the cars.

I turn my head looking around the grounds.

"Don't do it Josip." Sven says from behind me.

"Don't do what? What is he doing?" Luka asks.

"I'm not doing anything. I'll see you guys tomorrow."

"You are doing something; you're looking for that woman. I don't know who she is, but you need to get her the fuck out of your head." Sven says as he walks past me.

"What woman? There's a woman?" Luka asks still completely bewildered.

"There's no one." I can feel myself getting angry, though I know there is nothing that I would be able to do about it. They both out rank me in the family and I have to remain respectful in any situation. It's not usually hard to do, but the fact that Sven keeps jabbing me about being hooked on Bella is really starting to grind at me. "I'll talk to you tomorrow."

Sven turns quickly and glares at me, "No, you'll come with us to mingle." he softens his voice and shakes his head slightly, "Josip, I don't know why you choose to separate yourself from us so much. Are you annoyed by our company? We all must work together to keep a good relationship with the De Lucas, but it seems as though you are more concerned about being hidden."

"You're ridiculous. I don't mind being around the two of you, or anyone else in our family, but I can't stand the phoniness of these people and most other families. They are dragging us around town, smiling in our faces, making sure we are comfortable when I know for certain the second there is a chance that we are no longer of use to them, they will be right there to cut our throats. There is no loyalty, so why fake it."

A drop of wisdom comes from behind me, "Have you never heard of the fucking saying, keep your friends close, but your enemies closer? They are not the only ones who would be ready to kill if the need arises. Right now, there is no bad blood between our families, but I know I'd want to be the first one to find out if there were. They aren't family and never will be. Just because we are smiling back at them doesn't mean that we've forgotten that." Luka claps me on the back and walks off towards his brother. Sven and Luka are adopted brothers and even though they couldn't be more different, their bond is stronger than most blood brothers I've ever met.

"One fucking drink, and I'm not smoking anything." I sulk and follow the both of them into the small sitting room.

Four drinks later I'm feeling way more at ease with the people around me. I keep my composure, not letting the liquid courage cause me to look sloppy. A man whose name I've already forgotten is talking to me about a resort that he is planning on taking over in Columbia, an easy front to get drugs from one point to another.

A simple flash of long brown hair and a quick movement at the window is enough to have me forgetting everything that Sven and Luka had told me earlier, enough to make me forget that I'm in the middle of a conversation. I saw someone pass by the window in the direction of the garden and though I'm supposed to be staying away from Bella, I have to know if it's her. I need to know why she ran. I dart out the room and from the corner of my eye I can see Sven shoot me a severe look. He must know where I'm running to. I never run; I don't need to.

I race out the house to the garden and just like last night she's there. Instead of the dress she wore yesterday, today she is in tight jeans and a simple t-shirt. Her jeans accentuate the curve of her ass and her long legs, and just that easily, I want to touch her.

She combs a hand through her hair and lets her head fall back. She rolls her shoulders a few times and I hear her take a deep breath. She's tense about something, I can't help but wonder if she's upset that I'm not there.

I take a few steps in her direction before I call out her name. I don't want to startle her and I know she may have a hard time seeing me in the dark.

"Bella."

She gasps and turns around. "Josip, what are you doing here?"

"You know exactly what I'm doing here. I'm here for you. What the fuck happened yesterday? Why did you run off like that?" I take another few steps in her direction, but when I reach out for her, she puts a hand out to stop me.

"Josip, what we were doing yesterday can't happen again. You don't understand."

I shove my hand in my pockets and sigh, "No shit. I wish you would tell me what the problem is so I could understand." If she isn't engaged or attached to anyone here, there should be no reason why she should be so against what had happened between us. I know she liked it. I can remember clearly how she was moaning and rubbing against me.

"I may not be attached to anyone or promised, but I'm still off limits. I'll never be with anyone, it's punishment for who my mother was."

"Who was your mother?"

She rolls her eyes and throws her hands up in the air before she turns and tries to walk away, "Why the hell does it matter Josip? We can't do this. That's that."

I quickly catch up to her and grab her by the arm. I turn her, pulling her hard into my chest. "That's not that. I know you want more. I can feel how fucking bad you want me. It's the same for me. Tell me you want me to go away." I thread my fingers in her long hair and pull her head back, my cock already hard and the liquor making me bolder than I ever would be. "Tell me you don't want to feel me deep inside of you and I'll stop chasing you."

"Josip. We'll get in trouble." The warning barely audible falling from her lips.

"I won't tell if you don't." I smirk at her and lean forward. Before my lips can even come in contact with hers, she throws her arms around my neck and pulls me into a desperate kiss. There is no talking tonight, only our hands tugging and exploring each other.

4

Josip

It's months of us sneaking around like this.

Every time Sven or anyone else has to have a meeting with the De Luca family I suddenly need to go to Texas at the same time. Bella is very tightlipped as to why she'd get into trouble if anyone finds out about us. I don't press her, at this point I'll take whatever information she is willing to give me if it means that I get to keep seeing her. I've never felt so consumed by a woman in my life. A woman who understands when I won't be able to show up for a certain event or when I'm having a bad day and can't talk about it. Bella is everything that I could have ever wanted.

I've been sneaking to see her for about 2 months and it doesn't even bother me that we haven't had sex yet. I can say the urgency to have her tripled when she told me she was a virgin. Now, all I can think about is being the first one to bury myself deep inside of her.

To do that though would mean I would have to sneak inside the house with her.

"You're driving me crazy, Josip." Bella scratches her nails against my back as she grinds herself down on me. We are in the garden and she is straddling me on one of the benches. We might both still be clothed, but I can feel the heat coming off her.

"Tell me the fuck about it. I haven't been this pent up since I was a teenager." I sigh and push her slightly from my lap. I was at the point of no return.

She slides off my lap and sits down next to me, her eyebrows cinch in and she fiddles with the hem of her shirt.

"What is it?"

"Pent up? You mean you're not seeing anyone else?" She turns her gaze up to me.

"Nemoj me jebat!" I stare at her for a few seconds to see if she is indeed fucking serious, "Why the hell would I be seeing someone else? I thought we were doing this shit together. Are you seeing someone else? Because I don't need to be running around like a fucking creep if you're off with another man." I go to stand up and leave. "If there is one thing that I won't stand, it's sharing my woman."

"Josip! Stop it! I'm not with anyone, I just didn't think

25

you'd be exclusive to me. That's not what I was expecting." She grabs hold of my arm and pulls me back down. "Don't get so jealous."

"Fuck that, if you're my woman then you're my woman. It's bad enough I can only see you once or twice a month and even then, have to hide when we do. I'm not going to share you as well."

"Never, I'm yours as long as you want me." She drapes a leg over my thigh and pulls me closer to her. I'm still mad, but my need to touch her outweighs my need to be upset.

I stick my hand up her shirt and massage one of her supple breasts. She moans and rocks closer to me.

"You want to try something with me?"

"What?" I nip at her neck and let her grab me through my pants. "Fuck, what?"

"The pool house has an upstairs ... the cameras are broken. It's small, but there's a bed." I watch her gulp down hard. She's nervous.

"Take me."

She grabs my hand and we walk over to pool house, making sure to keep to the shadows. The pool house matches the white exterior of the main house, but it's hidden by trees. I can see that it needs a bit of upkeep, but I don't care about what it looks like. If she's comfortable I'd lay in horse shit right now to make love to her.

"Let me go in first and then when I turn the lights out come in. The cameras on the lower-level work, but not up top." Her breath is coming fast and she is looking from side to side as if she is waiting for someone to jump out of the bushes.

"Ok." I let her hand go and she hustles into the pool house. She's stealthy, slinking against the walls to stay out of the line of sight of the cameras. She stops every so often probably to give a camera the chance to pan, it seems as if she has done this quite a few times.

After a minute or so the lights go off and I quickly make my way inside the pool house.

"Josip." She whispers harshly.

"I'm here."

"I can't see you at all. You have to come to me."

I stay as close to the walls as I can, the same way as she'd done until I am able to grab her hand. Once I latch on to her, she tugs me toward the stairs behind her. She quickly makes her way up. Once we get to the second level, she fiddles with what looks like a fuse box and the lights come back on. I look at the ceiling on the second floor and see the cameras are out of their casings and there are wires sticking out from them.

"Come, the room is here." She pulls me again and we walk into what looks to be a guest room. The windows are all hidden by the trees letting only a small bit of moonlight into the room.

She is still looking around, scared that she's going to get caught. "Bella, we don't need to do this." I try to soothe her.

"I want to. I've never felt this way about anyone, never had anyone feel the way you do about me. You're the one bit of good in my life that I've been able to keep. I want to do this." Her voice is strong and she grabs hold of my shirt, pulling me towards her for a kiss.

The kiss erases any hesitation that I have. I can't hold back any longer. I push her, never once letting my mouth leave hers, until we are at the bed. She squeals slightly when I grab the back of her knees and make her fall back. I strip out of my shirt and she quickly takes hers off as well. Her bra is a pale pink and almost the same color as her skin, especially in the dim light.

"I can't fucking wait to feel you around me. You're so fucking beautiful Bella." I grab her jeans and yank them down her legs, her panties sliding down with them.

Her pussy glistens with her arousal. I drop down to my knees and spread her legs apart. I want her completely open to me.

"Josip, please. It's too much. I need you."

"I'm right here." I kiss the top of her pussy, the small patch of trimmed hair wet with her juices. I push her legs apart more and flick my tongue out to swipe at her slit.

"Oh God." She moans and her hands slam down on the mattress.

I pull away slightly, "No Bella, my name is Josip. When I fuck you, you scream my name. Every time you don't, I'm just going to have to fuck you harder."

She stares down at me, her eyes widening a bit, but a smile curling her lips.

I swipe my tongue across her pussy again now moving the tip of it hard against the tight nub at the top. She rocks her hips on my face, I have to grab hold of her hips to keep her where I want her.

"Oh, oh, Josip, I'm coming." Her thighs tremble and I have to fight to keep her legs open. A small gush of liquid bathes my tongue as her body jerks and she pulls at the sheets. "Oh God, Josip!" She moans out loud. I pull back and with a flat hand smack her clit causing her to scream out in shock.

"What the fuck did I say?"

"Josip, Josip, it's so good." She mewls.

"Fuck, you're going to unman me before I even get inside of you." My balls are heavy and tight. When I pull down my pants, my cock springs up ready to go.

I stand back slightly for her to get a good view, but it dawns on me that with it being so dark in the room she may not be able to see all of me.

"Bella, sit up. I want you to touch me."

She does so immediately her hands hesitantly come up and land on my abs.

"Oh ... my ... wow." She runs her fingers over the ridges of my well defined six pack. I don't have much bulk to me which means my muscles stand out. I'm what most would call shredded.

"Hmm, wait till you get to the prize at the end of the

trail." I joke and revel in the feel of her hands on my body.

Her fingers trail down and though she's touched my dick through my clothes before, this would be the first time she's laid her hands on my bare cock. Her delicate fingers wrap halfway around the shaft and she softly runs her hand down the length.

"Oh fuck." Her head drops back so she can look up at me, the black of her pupils completely taking over the bulk of her clear blue eyes. "You ... you're going to hurt me."

I don't want to lie to her. When it comes to my dick, I'm not a small man and from what I see of her pussy she may have a hard time taking me.

"If you want to stop you have to tell me now. I don't know if I'll be able to once we start. I want you so fucking bad." I grab hold of her hand to jerk it back and forth on my dick.

"No, I want you. I'm ready." She uses her free hand to pull me back onto the bed. She opens her legs for me and I lay down on top of her. I almost curse out in relief when the tip of my dick makes contact with her wet opening.

"I'm going to go as slow as I fucking can, okay? I'll hold back as much as possible." I let her know and hope that she realizes that I'm on my last thread of will power.

"I trust you." She uses her leg to pull me in further.

I press into her slick folds and the thick head of my dick squeezes into her narrow opening. The warmth is overwhelming and I find myself pushing forward harder than I want to.

She screams out in pain and her body clenches down pushing me back out. She still hasn't torn. However, if just getting this much into her is causing her that much pain I'm not sure she's going to be able to handle me ripping into her.

"Shhh, I'm sorry. Stay with me ok. I'll go slower." I whisper against her ear. When her body relaxes and she wraps her arms around my midsection again I push back in, this time moving at a snail's pace. She whimpers as I rock and roll my hips trying to stretch her out. "That's my good girl. You're doing so fucking good." I kiss her neck and she moans deep enough it feels like a purr.

"Push down with your hips, help me. You can do it Bella." I say against her skin and she gasps. She does what I ask instantly and I feel my dick slowly getting deeper inside of her. Once the ridge of my cock is engulfed in the heat that is her pussy, I can't keep this slow pace.

"Fuck, Bella. I need to go deeper. I need it. K Vragu, tako si čvrsto. Ne mogu prestati. Jebati." I know she doesn't speak Croatian, but I can't help the words coming out of my mouth right now. She doesn't understand that I'm telling her how tight she is or that I no longer have the strength to keep this slow pace. I hope she can understand it through my body language. I grab hold of her waist and hold her down as I plunge hard into her. She moans loudly and her eyes slam shut. I feel the barrier, I feel it stretching, but not giving way. I push harder, tightening my grip on her waist that will surely leave a bruise. Again, I pull back and thrust hard, the tight ring tears slightly. I can feel it on my sensitive skin. Bella screams in pain, but I don't pull out, instead I lock my lips on hers and slam the rest of the way into her. Her virginity is gone in that instant. She screams into my mouth and her nails scratch down my skin. My head is spinning and I'm out of breath when I lift my face from hers.

"My good girl. You did it. You did it for me." I kiss her lips tenderly and she nods her head soaking up all the praise I'm giving her. "You want more? Can I move?"

"Yes, I think it's ok." Her voice is hesitant. She's still in pain, of course she'd be hesitant.

I pull back and thrust into her with less ferocity, but still at a quicker pace. It's like I can feel each ridge of her inner walls. She molds to me and milks my cock. After a minute or two I feel her starting to roll her hips in time with my motion.

"That's right Bella, fuck me."

Her mouth gapes open slightly and she rolls her hips faster spurring me to move at the same pace. We kiss and touch desperate to get our fill of one another. When her body stops moving and she grips the sheets, I know she's right on the edge of ecstasy.

"Oh Josip, I'm going to come. So good. Oh God!"

"Josip!" I reprimand her and slam into her hard. Much harder than I had done the entire time we've been fucking. She gasps loud and a mischievous twinkle glints in her eye.

"Fuck me like that again."

My balls pull up tight to my body and I know that I'm not going to last much longer, especially with her saying shit like that.

"You want it hard baby? I give my girl what she wants. As long as I get what I want in return. When you leak that sweet cum on my dick, you'll say my name. You hear me."

"Yes, please, more." She lays back, but before she is fully against the bed, I'm already thundering into her. I watch as her thin abdomen contracts hard and her body begins to shake.

"Oh shit, yes, yes ... yes." Her voice is hoarse, but I can still hear it.

"I can feel you, let go for me baby ... Come." I command as I'm a second from losing my battle to hold on for her.

"Josip, Fuck!"

The walls of her cunt slam down hard and I growl loud at the sudden intensity of it. Just as she is in the middle of her orgasm, I feel the first large wave collide with my body and I release my seed deep inside of her. I lay down completely on top of her and grind as deep as I can get as pulse after pulse of my orgasm ripples through me.

I lay there on top of her for a few minutes completely speechless, just trying to catch my breath. If I thought I was smitten before, now that I've had her, I know there is no way that I will ever get enough.

We stay wrapped in each other's arms for a short while before she starts to get antsy. Worried that someone is going to come find us. I know she said that her being alone was punishment, but I still don't understand.

We quickly clean up the best we can, luckily she didn't bleed too much and we are able to strip the bed. I slide my clothes back on and wait for her to wash up in the bathroom to the side of the room.

"You go on downstairs I have to cut the power."

I wait for the lights to go off and I hurry down the stairs. It only takes one step out the front door for me to realize that we'd fucked up.

A heavy metal object collides with the side of my head. I put my arm up to block any follow up attack. I lunge forward and grab whoever it is attacking me. I slam my shoulder into his gut. Once he bends down, I grab the back of his head and bring my knee up into his face several times.

I may never need to get violent, but it doesn't mean I

don't know how to gut a motherfucker like a fish. I ball my fist up and swing hard at the man's temple causing him to drop to the ground in a daze.

The metal object in his hand is a gun, he's here to kill me. He's in a suit, working.

"Josip! No!" I hear Bella hiss out from the side.

I take stock of my surroundings quickly. No one else is here but the three of us so she must be telling me not to kill this motherfucker. In the one second that I back up, he stands and points his weapon at me.

"What the fuck are you doing here?" spits out the man I now recognize as one of the security guards.

"What business is that of yours?"

"I could put a fucking bullet in your head right now. I asked you a goddamn question."

"If you have to shoot me then fucking do it." I take a step closer to him.

"No, this is my fault I was showing him the pool house. That's all." Bella rushes to stand in front of me.

"Oh, that is rich. Come, the both of you. I'm sure Mr. De Luca is going to want to know about your private tour." The security guard holsters his gun and motions for Bella to walk. She doesn't hesitate and I have to move quickly to get myself between the man and her.

I want to ask her what the hell is going on? I hate feeling like I might have just signed her death warrant. I need to know if I have to kill this man, but the way she is steadily walking towards the main house makes me think that she's not fearful of that extreme of a punishment.

The three of us walk in the house, I see Sven and Matej standing in the foyer. The meeting must have ended and they are ready to leave. That's why the security was looking for me. Sven's cold glare intensifies as he watches me walk behind Bella. He's always suspected that I was still running around with this girl, but he's never had any proof. I guess me and a mystery woman being escorted by security is more than enough proof.

"Što se događa?" Matej asks. He wants to know what is going on. Our alliance with the De Luca family is strong, but it would only take one crack to make it crumble.

"Nothing, everything is fine." I remark.

"The hell it is." The security guard states. Sven and Matej fall in behind and follow us to the back of the house. The security guard knocks on the door and waits to be called in. When he opens the door I see Andrea, Leo, and Christian sitting completely unaware that anything is amiss.

"Is there a problem?" Andrea stares at Bella.

"I found the two of them coming out of the pool house." The security guard says simply before he steps to the side.

"I was just showing him the ..." Bella starts on the

same lie she'd told earlier, but Andrea's backhand to her face is enough to stop her.

"Don't think me a fool girl." He growls at her. "I'll deal with you later, but you ..." He focuses his attention on me. "You disrespect me in my home?"

"Disrespect, I have no idea what you mean by that."

"Josip, quiet." Sven takes a step in front of me. "Mr. De Luca, I'm not sure what is going on and from what I know I don't think Josip does either. There's no disrespect."

"Is this true? Does he not know who you are?" Andrea looks back to Bella.

"No. We haven't done anything." She lies again. We did a lot. I stare at the side of her face almost willing her to turn to me. She doesn't even twitch in my direction.

"I hope not. Josip, this is Orabella De Luca. My daughter."

My eyes whip to the older gentleman.

Bullshit.

"What?" I can't fucking believe it, there is no way. I know all of his children. That shit is a lie.

"Jebote." Sven curses under his breath and drops his head down.

"Her whore of a mother tried to trap me. When I tossed her out with the trash, she came back nine months later with a fucking baby. She's my blood, it's the only reason I haven't completely done away with her. But under no circumstances will I allow her to be used against me."

Piece by piece everything starts to fall into place. Why she was always on the grounds, why she was so sure that she would get punished if she were to be with anyone, and finally why she walked in here as if she knew she wouldn't be killed. She is a mob boss' daughter. An illegitimate daughter, but still his daughter none the less. She was completely right when she said that there was nothing that we could do that would allow us to be together. I am just a lowly bookkeeper and she, a powerful pawn in her father's empire.

"There is no disrespect, I didn't know." I say out loud so that Andrea De Luca hears me.

"Now you do. I hope that means this is the end of it. I would hate for our long-term arrangement to come to an end, because you want to run off with some whore's daughter." Andrea looks pointedly at me as if he were expecting me to answer him. I wasn't going to fight with him. I know how Mr. Juric acts with his children and Mr. Vavra and the Sever family. What they say goes.

"No, we would never do anything like that. All we can do now is offer up our sincerest apologies." Sven says from behind me. I clench my fists at my sides. I wasn't sorry in the least. I don't want her to think that I regret one moment with her. In reality, the stolen moments that I had with her were the best in my life.

"That's good to hear. Very good. Now, with all this

behind us I hope that we never have to address this matter again?" Andrea looks to me before he looks over to his son, he's the one that runs the De Luca family now. If he were dissatisfied with the outcome of this meeting then he can have me killed or worse. If he thinks I intentionally disrespected him then he could end all dealings with the Juric family.

Basically, my future hedges on whether he believes that I wouldn't try to pursue Bella again.

"Yes, I believe we have everything in order here." Leo glares at me for another second before he turns to look at whatever paperwork is on the table.

"We'll be on our way." Sven grabs me hard by the shoulder and turns me around. I turn my head in Bella's direction, but she doesn't look at me. Just a brief eye contact is enough to start up the entire discussion again, she's playing it safe as she should.

The second we make it out of the house I shake Sven off.

"Josip, what the fuck is your problem?" He bellows at me, clearly the anger of almost having to fight with the De Lucas still heavy on his mind.

"Sven, for fuck's sake I said that I didn't know. I thought she was a fucking worker here."

"Josip. I may not know much, but that seems like one of the first questions that someone in your position would ask. When did you start seeing her anyway?" Matej asks.

"Does that matter?" I reply not wanting to tell them that this secret relationship had been going on for weeks.

"No, it most certainly does not." Sven steps in front of me, "Josip, I've never once had to pull rank on you. You've never been the type to go against the grain, but this shit is so fucked up. I'm going to say this one time and I want you to hear it well. You will never seek this woman out again. If you see her in passing you will act like she doesn't exist. We've worked too damn hard to get on solid ground with the De Luca family to have some silly crush destroy it all." He stares at me waiting for a response. "Do you understand me?" He barks when I give him nothing. I nod once and begin to walk to the car.

I run a hand over my face, the smell of Bella still lingering on my fingertips. I commit it to memory.

Now that I know what kind of beast I'm dealing with I will take better precautions. I understand that it is forbidden for me to pursue Bella, but that doesn't mean that I'm going to stop. I know what we have is real and even if I have to keep her secret from the world, I'm not going to give up on her that easily.

5

JF

Josip

Present Day

THE NEWS that I'm needed at the De Luca meeting is nothing out of the ordinary with all that has been going on with Yemen and his auctions being brought down, many contracts have to be updated. It also means that I'm going to be able to see my girl. Over the past two years we've become much better at hiding and getting around—secret cell phones, blackmailing servants and drivers. There are even times depending on the guard that she is able to sneak off and stay at a hotel with me over night. The family doesn't really seem to care for her, the only reason she's under such intense protection is because she has the De Luca blood running through her veins.

Otherwise, she is expendable.

I hope that it gets to a point where they realize that she isn't a threat to their family and they release her. To me.

"Josip, you with me?" Matej waves a hand in my face, I must have zoned out.

"Yes, I'm here. Did we discuss what the new timeline would be?" I focus on him.

"Not yet, that's one of the main reasons I need you there. This contract could take a bit longer than Leo would like. I don't want there to be any misconception. I need it all laid out in black and white that there may be a delay." Matej is a bratok for the Juric family, while some would call him a jack of all trades, he specializes in human trafficking. Sometimes it's for sex slaves, other times it's for associates stuck in a different country that need to get past borders without the authorities finding out. So far, I have yet to see him fuck up.

"I'll be sure of it." I input a bit more information into my iPad to update the agreement that he will be talking with the De Lucas about. "Are you flying back out after your meeting or do you have other business to take care of here?"

"I'll be staying, you?"

"The same, I have some business to take care of." I can't fucking wait. I've already reached out to Bella and she is going to meet me at a hotel. It's been more than a month since I've been able to lay my hands on my woman. I know when we get together later tonight it's going to be explosive.

"Yeah, I bet you do have some business. You're a fool." Matej scoffs and leans back in his seat, closing his eyes in the process. No one knows for sure that I'm still messing around with Bella or if they do, they don't care enough to say anything. Part of me wants to think that if they do know, they don't say anything because they want me to be happy. Even though they are all ruthless killers they respect me enough to let me have her.

I don't engage Matej for the rest of the flight. I don't think about anything else besides finally being with my woman.

* * *

"OH JOSIP, I missed you so much." Bella attacks me the second I walk in the door to our hotel room. She'd managed to convince one of the guards that we have a little dirt on that she wouldn't be missed. I get to be with her all night long.

"Fuck, me too Bella." She kisses down my neck and threads her fingers in my hair. She pulls back and looks me in the eyes.

"You know you don't have to do this right? We can't keep this up."

"Don't start this again." I bend down and nip at her lip. She's always trying to get me to stop coming to her. The first time I was able to make contact with her after her father had warned me off, she thought I was out of my mind. She cried and begged me to stay away. She laughed at the fact that I was brave enough to even attempt something as crazy as this. Then, once she realized that I wasn't going to give up, she began to work with me to find ways to get around the huge obstacle that we would face while we are together.

Yet every time I'm able to visit her she makes sure to try and talk me out of coming back.

"Josip, you ..."

I seal my lips on hers once again to stop her from talking. There is nothing that she could say that is going to change how I feel. I'll do this for the rest of my life if I have to.

She peels my dress shirt off my body and I pull her t-shirt over her head. It feels like I can't get her naked fast enough. I pick her up and drop her on the bed. Her pants are still on, but she pops back up and sits on the edge.

"I want to taste you." She licks her lips and begins to tug at my belt and pants.

"I'm all yours Bella." I quickly toe my shoes off while she is still working on my pants and groan out in absolute pleasure when her warm mouth encloses my cock. "Fuck." I groan as my back arches slightly.

I'm the only one that Bella has ever been with which means I have been able to train her to meet every single need I could ever have and then some that I didn't even know about. I was never a really huge fan of getting my dick sucked, but whenever she gags on me, I have to stop myself from breaking to pieces. Each and every time.

I pump into her mouth and she looks up through her long lashes at me. "There's my good girl, I'll never get enough of you." I trail my thumb down her cheek my cock pushing the thin tissue to bulge slightly. I pull her back after I feel my knees buckle slightly. A long trail of spit connects my cock to her mouth. She daintily wipes her mouth with the pads of her fingers as if she didn't just give me a sloppy blowjob in a hotel room. I love that I'm the only one who will ever be able to see this freaky side of her. Whenever she's home, she's the epitome of grace and poise, but with me she's nasty and ready to try anything to please me. I'm the same for her.

I reach and yank her pants off. As I peel her panties down, I can see how wet she is for me, ready for the taking.

I want her to give me all she has. I want to be able to see her face as she is breaking apart on my mouth. I crawl over to the other side of the bed and lay flat on my back. She gives me a strange look, confused as to why I'm moving away from her.

"Come over here." I put my hand out and she crawls

over to me ready to sit on my hard and pulsing cock. She raises her legs and tries to straddle me, but that isn't what I want, not yet. "No, sit on my face."

Her eyes open wider and her cheeks turn a deeper shade of red.

"Ok." She squeaks out and quickly positions herself on my mouth. In this position I can completely devour her and she can fuck my tongue any way she wants. I suck and pull at her clit with my mouth as she grinds and swirls her pussy on my face. She tries to keep herself slightly elevated probably worrying about whether or not I'll be able to breathe, but I pull her down so she is flush with my face. I don't want her holding back not even for my well-being. Her juices drip down my throat and I drink them like it's the finest champagne. Her movements begin to become jerky as her body races towards her release.

"Oh, fuck Josip, wait. God!" She cries out and tries to lift herself up, her cunt pulsing on my lips as she comes. I swat her ass hard and pull her back down on my face. Even to this day, she has problems not saying God while I'm fucking her. I'm grateful for it. I slurp up the last bits before I flip her down onto the bed and thrust my dick completely inside her to the base in one swift motion. She cries out and claws at me. I don't care. She knows the rules, if she calls out for God, I'll just have to fuck her hard enough that she remembers it's me destroying her. I set a punishing pace, lifting one of her legs so her knee is lined up with the crook of my elbow. She drops her hands to the bed and gets a grip on the sheet to keep herself rooted to the spot and keep my thrusts deep inside of her. "Bella, you love it when I'm this deep inside of you. You feel me pushing at all your walls, your cunt's milking me dry?" I grunt out and she moans in reply. She swirls her hips as I pump into her.

"Josip, I'm close. Oh fuck. Don't stop. Yes ... oh Josip." she praises me. I have to shoot her a smile since she'd stopped herself from saying God. My hair is heavy with sweat and it flops down on my forehead in front of my eyes. I have to comb it back with my hand so it doesn't impede my sight of her. I love to see the way her body completely surrenders to me as I bring her to climax. Just as I feel the first contraction ripple through her walls, I bring my hand down to her cunt. Using her own arousal as lubricant I quickly rub my hand against her clit causing her orgasm to rocket to the next level. She speaks in tongues as her body jerks and rolls through the orgasm.

Her nails dig into my wrists, I hiss out in pain and drop down so I'm lying on top of her. She winds her arms around my neck and holds on as I piston into her. Every time I come, it feels better than the last with her.

Pins and needles erupt all over my skin and I groan into her neck as I feel my body on the very edge. Right now, all I can think about is how badly I want to come. How badly I want to be buried deep inside of her when

I shoot my seed. How I want this every day and not just when the both of us could sneak away.

"I love you Josip, so much." She whispers right above my ear. My body shakes with sensation from both the orgasm shooting through me and the intensity of my feelings for this woman. Once the bright spots dim from my eyelids, I lean up to look in her eyes. "I love you too Bella."

I don't know what I need to do to make her mine, but it's time that I figure it out.

6

Bella

My eyes are lined red from all the tears I've cried so far on my way back to the house. I had to leave Josip at the hotel in order to get back to the grounds before Leo or Christian were back from their meetings. Not that either one of them would come looking for me, but if I weren't there, they would want to know what was going on. I'm still forbidden from being with anyone romantically, but Leo is much less of a tyrant then our father. He turns a blind eye to certain things that Andrea would have never let me get away with. The last thing I want is for Leo to take back the small bit of generosity that he's shown me over the past couple of years, because he thought I was going behind his back.

I hate leaving Josip. Hate knowing that if anyone

were to catch us together it could cost us his life or mine. Hate that just because my mother was a gold-digging whore, I'm doomed to live this life. I didn't ask for any of this, hell if I could renounce the De Luca name I would. Unfortunately, that will never happen. I'm stuck living under lock and key until my death. Josip doesn't deserve that. He's such a good man—loyal to his family, attentive, sexy as hell. Everything I could ever want, yet a few hours a month is all I can ever give him.

"Orabella, you need to get yourself together before we get back to the house. Leo isn't back yet, but the rest of the staff is up taking care of their chores."

I nod my head and suck in a few cleansing breaths, but that only spurs more tears.

Timothy sighs softly and pulls out a handkerchief for me. I dab my eyes and do my best to calm down. Timothy is one of the guards that Josip was able to dig up dirt on. Apparently, years ago he used to be part of a gang of people who'd kidnapped my cousin Sloane. He didn't have anything to do with it, in fact he didn't even know about it, but Leo has been going crazy trying to take care of any loose ends. He wants to irradicate the entire group of them no matter if they had anything to do with it or not. If Josip ever let it slip that Timothy used to even associate with those bastards Timothy would be in for a long and painful death. Josip and I had made a deal with Timothy that he would assist in getting me in and out of the house when he could. Covering for me when need be. I didn't expect him to go out of his way, but most of the time he did. I didn't know if it were because he was truly scared of what Leo would do or because we had developed a bit of a friendship. I think Timothy felt bad that Josip and I had to sneak around.

"Thank you, Timothy. I'm ok now." I hand him his handkerchief back and do my best to settle myself. There was nothing that I can do about my puffy red eyes, but hope that no one sees me.

The car pulls into the driveway and I get out not waiting for him to escort me in. The second I walk into the large house, I see Leo walking right towards me.

"Where the fuck have you been?"

Panic sets in as I think that maybe he knows about me going off to meet Josip. "I just went for a little early morning walk. Timothy was with me. He's right outside."

Leo squints his eyes at me, "What are you crying about then?"

I chuckle and do my best to play it off, "I saw a litter of kittens, they were dirty and small, I didn't see their momma which made me think they were all alone. I felt bad for them and all of a sudden, the waterworks. I'm due for my time of the month any day now." PMS, one subject most men shy away from.

"Yeah, whatever. Get in the house. I don't want you

off the grounds again until I say so, you understand?" Leo's voice is cold and straight to the point. I wouldn't say that he is the most approachable person ever, but something else is happening to cause him to act like this.

"Is everything ok?" I press. I have no place asking him anything about business, but if whatever is happening requires me to be quarantined to the house then maybe he would give me a hint.

"No, I don't think so. Something is happening. Something big, but I don't know all the details. One of Ilia Vavra's daughters is missing. They think it's a kidnapping."

I gasp and take a step closer. That is really fucking bad. Ilia Vavra is the leader of one of the strongest Croatian crime families. "Oh, do you think it's a power play?"

"I don't know what it is. All I know is I don't want to take any chances. We won't negotiate with anyone." He stops short, but I know exactly what he is thinking about saying next. He won't negotiate with anyone especially for me.

This is my life. I am too important to let go, but not important enough to fight for. Stuck in a perpetual state of unworthiness. I don't have any information that anyone would want and since I will never hold any place of power in our family, they'd rather let me be someone's hostage then use any resources to get me back.

"I understand. I'll stay put." I give him an encouraging smile and walk off towards my own room. There is nothing else that he will tell me anyway.

I move past the guards that are standing in front of my room and close the door behind me as I relax in my small space. I have a bed, a desk, and a bathroom. The TV and laptop are my only forms of entertainment while I'm here. It's truly amazing how I didn't go crazy from boredom years ago.

I lay down on the bed and pull one of the pillows to my chest. These four walls are all I have and even those aren't mine. Until I started with Josip, I didn't realize how much I crave freedom. Now, the thought of being stuck here for an undisclosed amount of time is maddening.

I pull out the phone I have hidden in the bed post and shoot Josip a text wishing him a safe flight. After I put it away, I roll over to the side and smell my hair. It smells of him. Hopefully, he'll be waiting for me in my dreams.

7

Josip

Fucking chaos.

    That is the only way I can describe what I came back to in Las Vegas. Matej and I took off early this morning, but the second my phone's in range the messages and calls start to roll in. An emergency meeting called and Mr. Juric wants everyone to meet at the Košnica. I don't know what it is about, but from the sound of Sven's voice, something major must have happened. We get off the plane and drive the car straight into the heart of Las Vegas. The Košnica, or the hive, runs under the strip. The best place to hide anything is right under your nose.

    "Josip, I trust everything is in order with the De Luca deal?" Sven says the moment I walk into the large banquet room that Marko tends to use for his meetings.

There is a large spread of food and quite a few guests already sitting waiting for the meeting to start.

Sven, Luka, Liam Juric, Dominik, and Katarina Juric sit at the table as they are all high-level members of the family. Dagger, one of the best hitmen in the world along with Kaja and Zelimir, who are both vors, stand off to the side speaking amongst each other. It's very rare that so many of us are called together at one time.

I give Sven a nod to let him know that everything is taken care of.

Marko Juric comes out of the restroom and instantly all the talking dies down. When the Pakhan enters everything stops.

"Obitelj, I have concerning news." Marko speaks and sits down in his chair in the center of the table. "We have someone who is going after important members of other families, possibly coming for us. The women." He stops talking to let that sink in.

"Do we have any clue as to who may be doing it?" Luka asks.

"Not a clue."

"I think we should put a hold on any contracts." I say immediately. If there is someone coming for us or our associates than we need to keep everything locked down.

"I completely agree with that. If they think that we are going to be able to run around and get things done with contracts at a time like this they must be crazy. It would be like us leaving our own women out to be taken. We need to make sure that we are all available in case whoever this is decides to try and come for one of us. Though I don't think anything like that will be happening. I think that maybe this focuses on the Vavra family." Sven says from where he is sitting across from Marko.

There's no information yet, but I'm sure that he would get it. Especially if it meant that he would be able to protect Ema. I had heard stories about men being super protective over their loved ones, but Sven is the extreme. If there were ever a reason to keep her locked up in his house, I'm sure that he would take it.

"No, business will go on as usual. If someone is dumb enough to come after us then we will be ready, but we are not going to let some outside fucks dictate how we run our business. We do what we have to do to keep everything running smoothly, but if you find out any information about what is going on of course we all need to know. Luka, I need you to take point on this. This is a security matter and we need to make sure that all of our families are properly watched over. If you find any lags in security, make sure to rectify it." Marko says as he picks up a Danish and stuffs it in his mouth. How the man isn't five hundred pounds I don't know. He's always eating.

"Da, as you wish." Luka nods his head and clamps his mouth shut. If I don't know any better it would seem as if he doesn't agree with his dear old father. That's a first at least for me. Luka is the carefree one of us, if there were anyone that I think would give more pushback it is Sven.

"Josip, you will go over all of our contracts and agreements, make sure that this will not impede anything. We have to remain strong; do you understand?"

"Yes sir." I nod and wait for Marko to give the next directives.

As he goes around the room giving orders to everyone here, I think back on what I was doing just hours ago and a twinge of fear blossoms in my gut. What about Bella? Would she be safe enough where she is? I know that she is in the De Luca family's care, but they rarely check in on her. So many things could go wrong and there would be no way for me to get in contact with her besides the phone. It's times like this I wish I could just keep her locked away in my own closet. I know for sure she would be safe with me. For now, I have to rely on Leo and Andrea De Luca to keep my woman safe.

* * *

WITHIN THE NEXT WEEK, three more women are stolen. Another two associates from the Vavra family and one from the Sever family. Shit is getting bad and everyone is on edge. I stop by Sven's home for our weekly meeting and he greets me at the door looking like he hasn't slept in days.

"You look like hell. Are you sick?"

"No, someone tried to break in yesterday, luckily my cameras caught them in the act and we woke up. I think they were here for Ema. I can't fucking think about shit right now. I need to get her out of here. I have to keep her safe." He runs a hand through his hair and I watch as a very heavily pregnant Ema wobbles down the stairs, another reason for his crazy behavior. Ema is carrying his first child, a little girl.

"Sven, I'm fine. We are going to be fine. You know that. I don't want to be anywhere besides where you are." She says quietly from behind him.

He turns in shock that she's behind him and rushes over to where she is. "What are you doing up? You should still be in bed."

"Your child decided it was time to get up. I didn't really have a choice." She laughs and reaches out for him. The simple intimate interaction between the two of them is enough to make me want to turn my head and give them privacy. They are still very much in the honeymoon phase of their marriage.

"Did you reach out to Luka yet?"

"Yeah, he's in the back trying to add in a few more cameras so that I'll be able to see more. There are guards back there with him, but none of that shit matters to me.

What the fuck is a camera going to do if someone comes in here?" Sven turns back in my direction. He's losing his shit.

"I don't know Sven, but we have to keep a cool head, whoever is doing this is trying to get us to fuck up. Take everything one step at a time. Any luck with the other kidnappings?" I put my briefcase down on the couch, whatever we had needed to discuss today is now put on the backburner. He's not going to be able to focus on anything besides keeping Ema safe. The least I can do is give him someone to bounce ideas off of.

"That's the shit. I've got nothing. There are no whispers of it on the dark web. No ransoms. Nothing ... just fucking women up and disappearing." He runs his hand through his hair again and Ema rubs his back trying to console him.

"What about past allies, maybe one of the families that we have broken ties with has come back for vengeance?" It's so strange to have to talk about anyone coming after the Juric family and succeeding.

"Nothing. Fucking nothing."

My phone vibrates in my pocket indicating that I have a text message. When I pull it out, I see that it's from Bella. I have to clench my jaw to keep myself from smiling.

"My love, *how are you this morning?*"

"Busy. Do they have you properly protected at the house?" I shoot back immediately. I've asked her the same thing every day this week if she's within reach of a guard or family member.

"Yes, Josip. Everything is fine. I promise you."

I can almost hear her chuckling; she always thinks I'm over-exaggerating about things.

"It's not fine and I'm not going to calm down until this shit is dealt with."

"I know it. When do you think I'll be able to see you again?"

"I don't know. Fuck I wish you were here. With everything that is going on, Mr. Juric is demanding that as many people as possible stay close. We aren't stopping any of our on-going deals, but we aren't making any new ones at the moment. So, I have to stay put. If they call for me and I'm not here that could be an issue." I do my best to explain to her why I'm not going to be around.

"I know ... part of me wanted to think that you would say tomorrow, but that's just hopeful wishing."

"I wish I could be there with you right now."

"I know."

"Josip, who are you talking to?" Ema asks from behind Sven.

"Hmm? What happened?" My head pops up and I slip the phone back in my pocket.

"You have a pained look on your face. You, ok?" She turns her head to the side.

"Yes. I'm fine, thank you for your concern."

"Look who's here." Kaja and Luka walk in from the back of the house and Kaja makes his way over to me. Out of everyone I'm the closest to Kaja. Though he is just a lower class vor, he is loyal to the family and will do anything to make sure that we come out on top. He is also always on the very tail end of everything. Never able to get too far into what is happening, because he is only a made man and not a bratok. They treat him like a glorified errand dog.

"Kaja, what are you doing here? Are you going to be helping out with security?" I shake his hand and then reach over to shake Luka's. Luka only gives me a slight nod before he walks over to his brother.

"No, Luka just needed someone to help him install a bit of equipment. Someone from inside the family."

"Ah, seems like you are handy to have around in a tough spot." I joke with him. "What about Sabina? Is everything ok with her?"

"She's fine, I've left her with her brother for the time being. How did everything go over at the De Lucas?"

I simply shrug my shoulders. There is no need to go into any extra details.

At the same time there is a round of vibrations that go off around the room. Every single one of our phones receiving a notification at the same time.

"Jebote!" Sven yells out when he looks at his phone.

I pull mine out and there is one message. The same one I'm sure that Sven and the rest of the people here got. Katarina Juric, Marko Juric's daughter had been kidnapped.

Now this isn't just someone coming for our allies. No, this is someone coming after us. I don't know who is dumb enough to start a war with all of us, but that is exactly what they just did.

8

JF

Bella

I've been locked up in the house for a full two weeks straight now.

Everyone is on edge. Even Josip is trying to think of ways to sneak me out so that I can be with him. I do what I can to reassure him through the phone, but it's starting not to work. It's well past nine at night, but I just don't think I can force myself to go to sleep. I pace back and forth in my small room literally bouncing off the walls from boredom.

"I need to get the hell out of here. Just for a few minutes." I open my door and see that there is no guard standing out front. Probably out taking a piss. Perfect. I slip out and down the side stairs that only the help uses. It leads right out towards the garden. Even if it's just to smell the flowers for a little while I need to get out of here.

I take my time and stroll waiting for a guard to pop up at any second.

"Oh God, please. Help. Help." A weak voice comes from the back end of the garden where the hedges were high.

I stop in my tracks thinking that it might be a trap. Who the hell is out here? No one uses this garden, but me.

"Who's there?" I call out.

"Timothy ... Bella, is that you?"

Oh fuck.

I walk quickly in the direction of the sound of his voice, but I have to take my time. It's dark out and even with the few lights that are scattered along the outside of the house I'm already having a hard time seeing what's right in front of me. I find him on the ground with a large blade sticking out of his chest.

"Oh my God! Timothy what happened? Who did this?" I put a hand up to grab the knife, but think better of it before I do. I can see it tremble with his pulse. It's in the center of his chest, I don't know how close it is to his heart. I don't want to risk moving it and killing him in the process.

"I don't know, their faces were covered. They know the grounds. They are keeping to the shadows. There's two at least. You have ... to ... go ... inside. Find Christian or Leo. Sound alarm." His words are becoming more and more strained as a puddle of blood grows under him. I don't know what I can do to help him right now, but I can do what he asked and go back inside to let everyone know that we are being attacked.

His face is turning pale and his breaths are short. "Timothy, just hold on ok. I'm going to get help right now. Just don't die!" I feel a tear dropping down my cheek as I stand up and take off towards the exit of the garden. I turn the corner and no more than 50 feet in front of me is a person in all black, with an orange and red mask on their face. I scream and turn to run in the opposite direction.

My heart stutters and starts again at breakneck speeds. I haul ass down the east side of the garden thinking that I can get to the front of the house and get someone's attention.

"Help! Please!" I scream at the top of my lungs, but I don't stop running. I have to skid to a stop as I see the stairs to the front of the property, but standing in front of it is the man with the mask. How the fuck did he get there? He was right behind me.

Wait, Timothy had said that there were two of them, fuck they are keeping me from getting to the house.

I turn in the opposite direction and take off towards the pool house. Maybe I could get someone's attention from there. There's a phone, I could call to the main house. I run as fast as I can, my eyes not able to focus on anything and I trip a few times, but never fall. I know my way to the pool house with my eyes closed. With it being so dark, I will have to put that knowledge to the test. My feet finally come off grass and land on hard concrete letting me know that the door should be close by. All I can see right now is a large blob. I put my hands out and try to feel my way to the door. I can hear the pool water to the left so it should be right here.

"Yes!" I hiss out when my hand finally touches a doorknob. I push it open and safely make my way over to the stairs. I could flick on the lights, but that would just let them know that I'm in here.

The moonlight is enough to illuminate the rooms on the top floor enough for me to make out objects. I grab for the phone and put it to my ear. I don't hear anything. The line is dead.

What the fuck is this?

I click the receiver a few times, but still nothing happens.

"Here, pretty, pretty." A crazed voice floats through the air. It's coming from downstairs.

I suck in a breath and quietly hang the phone back up. There is no way for me to get out of here without going past whoever that is. I try to get my heart to calm down, but it feels as if it's going to beat out of my chest. I won't be able to fight whoever it is off and I have no idea if anyone has even heard me screaming for help.

All I can do right now is hide and hope that someone shows up before whoever the intruders are find me.

I look around. It's a pool house, there are not many options when it comes to hiding. I could go in the bathroom, under the bed or in the closet. All of these places seeming more cliche than the last. I choose the closet and quickly hide myself under a mountain of towels and pull a box in here closer to me so it looks as if someone had just been sloppy about throwing the dirty linen into the closet. It is dark enough in the closet that maybe I wouldn't stand out.

My entire body is shaking and I have to bite down on my knuckles to keep myself quiet.

"*Muñeca?* Where are you pretty girl?" The man calls out again. Now I can hear his footsteps slowly making their way down the hall. "I just want to play with you. Don't you want to be my friend? I'll make it worth your while, I promise." The man cackles at the end of his request and the sound heightens my fear. I've never heard this person before. I don't know who they are or what they could want from me.

Footsteps come into the room that I'm in and then they stop.

"Pretty girl. You're making me mad. I was going to be nice to you, but if you don't come out things are going to be very bad for you." His voice no longer has the sing song lilt it had moments ago.

I press my hand tightly to my mouth as I have to fight my body from letting out a whimper.

I can't see, I have no idea what he wants and no one has yet to come for me. I don't even hear anyone outside calling out for me. Is it possible that no one has noticed what is going on? Bigger tears stream down my face as I realize Timothy is most likely already dead.

I hear footsteps leave the room and almost laugh at my good fortune. I drop my hand from my mouth and let out the breath that I'd been holding. I don't move from where I am though. I'll just stay righ-

The door to the closet swings open and the towels are ripped away from my body.

"Oh, *Muñeca*, it's so good to see you."

My body seizes for a second. I'm so shocked that I don't know what to do. Thoughts of running, fighting or just screaming flash through my head in that microsecond. When the man standing in front of me pulls up a strange looking weapon the answer to what I'm going to do next is answered for me. I open my mouth and scream as loud as I can. The man pulls the trigger and something sharp hits me in my throat. My scream is cut short and I put my hand up to touch my neck. Something long and hard is sticking out of my neck. This isn't a bullet, it's a dart.

What the hell?

In as little time as it takes me to put my hand to my neck and let it fall back down again, the world starts to violently spin. I can no longer open my mouth to ask any questions. I can't speak, the numbness seems to radiate from my neck in waves. A whimper is all I can hear when I do try and speak. The lights dim even further and before I realize what is happening, the man in front of me is leaning down and picking me up from the closet. Darkness takes me as I listen to him sing a sweet song in Spanish.

    The De Luca family, they'll never come for me. This is it for me, I just hope Josip will be okay.

9

Josip

Marko is spitting mad. He has everyone going crazy trying to find out who took Katarina. Along with the attempted break-in to Sven's home we all know for sure now that this is an absolute attack. There is no coincidence about it. Still there has been no talk of a ransom or anyone taking responsibility for what is going on.

"Josip, none of this is recent." Sven pushes the computer away from him and back towards me. He wants to know the last few deals that Katarina had made. She may be a Juric, but as a woman she would never hold a high place in the family. Instead of being in a high position like Sven or Luka, Katarina is only a bratok, she handles all the small arms deals in the states.

She has been itching to branch out, but her father doesn't see the need. I think it's really because he wants to keep a short leash on her. Unfortunately, even with that short leash someone was able to come in and steal her.

"These are the last deals that she set up through me, if she made any other deals, it was under the table and not connected through the family. There hasn't been a lot of demand for the equipment that she has."

Sven narrows his eyes at me and pulls the computer back in front of him. "Have we looked into these contacts? Do their alibis check out?"

Luka is standing against the wall, a scowl on his face. "I already told you that I did that. I'm getting sick and tired of you double checking me."

Sven quickly turns and faces off with his brother, ready to fight if the need arose.

"Stop it. You both are worried. Everyone is going to double check everything until we find the connection." I pull the computer back and bring up any information that Katarina might want kept secret.

Anything that would mark her as a target.

Yeah, there were a few dings. She's had an abortion and killed an elected official, but nothing that would point anyone in the right direction.

Luka's phone rings, but I don't bother to pay attention. I'm still busy combing through information.

"Sven, Kaja is on his way here. Apparently, he was

able to get an update and a photo from one of the other kidnappings."

"What? Of who?"

"Petra Sever." Luka says and Sven squeezes his eyes shut. Petra is one of the first women that were kidnapped and she is Ema's cousin. When he found out that someone from Ema's family had been taken his possessiveness went into overdrive. I don't think Ema has left the house since all of this had started.

"It's verified?"

"I don't know brother. We have to wait until he gets here." Luka says, his voice softer than before. I've never heard them say that they love each other, but I'm sure Luka knows how much this is killing Sven.

I continue my task of looking for any connections. The problem with keeping all the records and having all the information is there is so much of it. I could go through the files for days and still not make a dent in it.

The doorbell rings a few minutes later and Kaja comes in. His face drops when he sees me sitting here.

That's odd. Last time we saw each other we were on good terms.

"Kaja, you have information?"

"Yeah, I got a photo off the dark web of whom I'm sure is Petra Sever. I can't clearly make out who is carrying her, but there is a bit of a profile view of him. Not the best quality." He pulls out the photo and lays it down on the table in front of Sven, both Luka and I get closer to see the image.

It is definitely Petra. She is in the arms of a man with her head and arms laying back and limp, clearly unconscious. The man is an average build in all black clothing, he has a mask that is pulled up to rest on the top of his head. It's red and orange. His hair is red as well from what I can tell. I study the small bit of side profile of the man's face, but I don't know him.

"Sranje!" Sven bangs his hand down on the table and pushes away. "Anyone know who that is?"

"No."

"Sorry." Luka replies after I do.

"Alright. I'll get this over to Marko, maybe he could reach out to some of his contacts. Spread the net wider." Sven puts his hands on his hips and paces slightly back and forth. "If this fucker is stupid enough to mess up already there is no way that he won't mess up again. Kaja, do you know who was able to pull this information?"

"No, I found it on a forum, specifically designated for people who take credit for hits. People are starting to whisper about massive changes happening within the families. It's a fucking mess."

"Shit, sharks are going to smell blood in the water. If it's this easy to attack us, others will try." Now it's Luka's turn to push away from the table. This whole shit show falls directly on him. He is the head of security for the entire family. Katarina shouldn't have been able to be kidnapped.

I look over to Kaja, but he deliberately looks away from me.

"What else? There's more." I speak up, knowing Kaja. Whatever he has to say he believes there will be some backlash for it. As a vor he has to be very careful about what he says and does.

Both Sven and Luka look up at him waiting for him to continue.

"I know these problems don't have anything to do with our family and I haven't been able to verify it, but there are rumors that there was another kidnapping last night. Along with a guard being killed."

"What? Who, I didn't hear anything?" Sven talks quickly.

I grip the arm rests of the chair and wait for Kaja to continue.

"Yeah, they only found out this morning." His eyes flick to me for a second before they go back to Sven, "Orabella De Luca was kidnapped last night and her guard Timothy killed."

Time stops.

No. Fuck no. No!

I suck in a ragged gasp. Everyone looks at me. "What the fuck are you talking about? What the fuck!" My voice gets louder with every word.

"I don't know the details; I just know what I read." Kaja puts his hands up and takes a step back.

"Josip, calm the fuck down." Sven says from where he is standing by his desk.

Red flashes in front of my eyes and if there wasn't a table in between us I would have lunged at him. "Calm down? No, I'm not going to fucking chill out. We have to find her. I need more information. What do they want?"

"Josip, she's not our family, not our responsibility." Sven yells back at me.

"She's mine!" I roar and swing my hand across the table causing the glass of water to go flying in Sven's direction. It crashes into the wall behind him, shards of glass and drops of water barely missing him.

"We fucking told you to leave her alone!" Luka says from behind me.

I turn to look at him, ready to take my anger out on him as well. When I look at him instead of hostility, I see sorrow painted on his face. I know what he knows. As much as I love her, she's not mine. She is still a De Luca and they have already told me under no circumstances will they ever let me have her. I can't go into the De Luca house and demand information. They could kill me just for having contact with her. I can't do anything for her, but pray that her family will try and get her back.

It feels like the walls are closing in on me. I take a

few steps until my back hits the wall behind me. For someone who normally has all the information to feel so lost is new and not a feeling I ever want to get used to. "I need to find her. I need her ... Please." I drop my head into my hands, I'm stuck.

Kaja is the first one to come over, the mammoth of a man who I've seen kill in a blink of an eye, wraps an arm around me and holds me off the wall. Luka comes next and puts a strong hand on my back. I've never been totally integrated into the family, always one or two steps outside. I have never even thought they considered me a friend, yet here the two of them stand supporting me like brothers.

"We have to do this behind Leo's back." Sven speaks, Luka and Kaja back away from me and my eyes bounce up to Sven. He is leaning against his desk with his arms crossed over his chest staring at me. "This is a project for the four of us, you understand. If Marko gets wind of this it'll be our asses. Josip, this shit is going to be hard, you need to keep your fucking cool or they are going to know. You went over a clear boundary. Marko nor Leo won't give a fuck about you loving that girl. She belongs to them. You went back on your word. If you start going crazy, they're going to know."

He is going to help me. "Alright, I'll keep it together. I'll do my fucking best. We need to move fast. If it happened last night maybe there are some security cameras that we could get some footage from."

"Not from the De Luca property. They'll know it's us looking at it and we'll look guilty as fuck." Luka says.

"What about the surrounding area? Maybe a traffic camera?" I scan through the possibilities in my head. They'd have to get her off the grounds, but once they were on the main roads it would be much harder for us to pinpoint them. We didn't know the make or model of the car. We didn't even know if they left on foot. All I know right now is that they took her.

"I can look into that. I might be able to piggyback into the De Luca system, but I can't guarantee it." Sven says as he walks back over to his desk to punch a few things into his computer.

"Ok, what should I do?" I look to the three of them.

"Work, make sure this family is straight. Find out what information you can about Orabella and just try to keep your head on right." Sven says.

"Go on, home. We'll let you know if we find anything. You have my word. Whoever has your woman also has our sister, so this is more than just a top priority, it's our only priority." Luka squeezes my shoulder before he walks over to his brother to help him.

"Come on, I'll leave with you." Kaja says and grabs hold of my arm. It feels like my feet are glued to the ground. "Come on Josip, there is nothing you can do here." I let Kaja lead me out the room. My entire body is tense like a rubber band ready to snap at any second.

I walk with him towards the car. He hasn't said a word about me going against the rules.

"I didn't have a choice." I remark.

"I know. You love that woman. We all know you do, but you need to realize that there is a real possibility that this isn't going to work out how you want. She's expendable in their eyes."

I open my mouth to retort, but Kaja cuts me off, "But I promise you I will do everything I can to get her back to you. Those guys in there too. If you love her, she's our family now and we never leave family behind."

My shoulders drop as I feel a bit of the weight that I had been holding onto just lift off me. They won't let me down. With or without the De Luca family's help we will find Bella.

10

Josip

Three days pass and two other women have been kidnapped. This time one is from the Bianucci family all the way in New York City. We had no allegiances with them, but the Don did reach out to Marko to find out if there was any information that he would be willing to give. It was no longer about keeping information secret, because we were in different families, now it was about finding our people. Allegiances be damned.

In those three days we haven't found any further evidence as to where they managed to take Bella. There was video of her running through the garden, video of what looked like a shadow of another person and then her running into the pool house. The lower level of the pool house was too dark for the cameras to pick up who had walked in and the cameras on the top floor were still not functional.

With so many different families being attacked Marko called for a sit down. He's asked for all of the leaders of our different allied groups to come and think up a plan on how to stop all these kidnappings.

I'm on auto pilot when I make my way into the Košnica. I wasn't explicitly invited to the meeting, but there is no way that I'm going to be able to stay home and just wait for someone to get back to me with information.

I see Wire and Keeley on their way out while I am walking in.

"Josip! Oh, are you ok?" Keeley pulls me into a hug the moment she lays eyes on me.

"Yeah. Why do you ask?"

"Honestly, you look like you have one foot in the grave." She takes a step back and looks me over again. I catch a glimpse of my reflection on one of the photos hanging on the wall and see immediately what she is talking about. My light blond hair is disheveled and clearly not combed, I have the makings of a very thick beard, and I think I misbuttoned my shirt. I look like Hell, none of that matters, all that matters is we are one step closer to finding Bella. We have to be.

"Yeah, it's been a rough few days." I turn my attention to her husband, Wire. "The meeting is over already?" I didn't expect anyone to be coming out yet.

"Yeah, ransoms have been sent out."

"What? For everyone?" So far, we hadn't received word from anyone about why our people were being taken. No one had asked for a thing. All of a sudden to have everyone get ransom requests at the same time seemed too coincidental.

"Yeah, folks are running off now to do what they need to do in order to get their people back."

She's coming back. I nearly jump out of my skin in joy. "Thanks! I have to get in there! Thanks!" I back away from him and turn before he even has a chance to say bye back. I knock on the door only barely remembering my place. If Mr. Juric is in there still conducting business, then it would be bad form for me to just barge in.

The door opens and I walk in not even bothering to see who opened it for me. Marko is still there speaking with Liam along with Sven and Luka. None of the bratoks were in attendance. I don't see Ilia Vavra or Ivan Sever. Most importantly, I don't see anyone from the De Luca family. It is just like Wire said, they had gone to get their people.

Sven and Luka walk over to me the second they see me.

"Josip, we did everything we could, you have to remember your place." Sven whispers to me. He stands right in front of me to block Marko from seeing me.

The words coming out of his mouth aren't making

sense. What does he mean they did everything they could? About what?

"What are you talking about? Wire said that everyone got ransoms."

"They did." Luka answers.

"That included Bella. Right?" My hands shake in anxiety.

Sven swallows hard before he continues, "Yes, but the De Luca family will not give them what they want. No swap will be made."

"Sranje! They can't fucking leave her there. They can't!" I yell in his face and rage erupts inside of me. "Where is that piece of shit Leo! Mother fucker!" I try to push my way around Sven, but both he and Luka grab me. They are already trying to get me out of the room.

"*Stani, što se događa?*" Marko asks from his chair.

"Nothing, it's fine." Sven says still trying to get me out of the way. I can see that Leo isn't in the room, but I can't stop fighting.

"I asked you a question Sven! What is going on?" Marko stands up from his seat and glares at us.

Sven lets me go, and I walk swiftly toward Marko. "Why isn't anyone going to negotiate for the release of Orabella De Luca?"

Marko's eyebrows shoot up to his hairline. "Orabella De Luca?" he takes his time and walks around the table until he's standing right in front of me. His arms cross over his chest and a slight scowl on his face, "Orabella

De Luca has nothing to do with this family, why should I concern myself with what they want to do with her?"

"It's my concern. I'll pay the ransom. Whatever it is." I offer immediately.

"Don't be silly boy. She's their property, besides it's not money that they are after. If Andrea and his family don't think the girl is important enough to go after, then she's just going to have to rot wherever she is. That's the life Josip, you know it."

"No! It's not!" I yell and step directly into Marko Juric's face. The sound of four guns cocking erupt around me.

Sven, Luka, Liam, and one of Marko's personal security all have their weapons pointed at me. I just completely disrespected my Pakhan. He doesn't say a word, just holds my gaze. His signature gold eyes burn into my soul.

I drop down to my knees immediately in front of Marko and drop my head in complete submission. "I beg your forgiveness. I've wronged you."

"How so?" Marko asks.

"I was told to stay away from Bella, but that was after I had already spent a significant amount of time with her. Love has no place in our world, but she's my woman. I will do anything to get her back. I never meant to cross you, but by the time I'd found out who she is it was too late."

"Josip, that is the daughter of –"

I cut him off, "I don't want anything. I'd never try to overthrow Leo or anyone over there. I don't want fortune or favor ... I just want my woman. They don't want her. They have no use for her. I mean ... they are just going to let some maniac have her, because they won't pay the ransom. Please, I beg you. We must convince them to get her. She doesn't deserve this."

Marko tsks, "Get up, Josip."

I stand and take a step back to give him some space.

"If it weren't for the years of loyalty and service that you've given me, I would be scooping your brain out of your skull. You've gone against your family and because of that I am hesitant to believe that I can trust you. If I can't trust you, what good are you?"

"Father!" Sven calls out from behind me.

"Marko, you can't! Not Josip. It's just a woman." Liam says from behind his brother.

"I don't care if it's a woman or a fucking dog on the street. This family comes before anything. If he is willing to go against our rules, he doesn't belong with us!" Marko yells at Liam before turning back to me, his face red with anger and his chest heaving up and down quickly.

"Josip, no longer will you claim the Juric name. No longer will the blood of my family be your seal of honor, you've disgraced my name and deserve nothing more than death." Marko glares at me for a second before walking back to his seat. "Luka, kill Josip and get his body out of here."

"Marko." I can hear the pain in Luka's voice.

"Marko, wait, I think we could be missing a grand opportunity here." Sven talks this time.

"How so?"

"Josip knows more information than any of us, and this last attack is still a mystery to us. Even if we give the bastards what they want we will never really know who is behind it. Give Josip the chance to get back in your good grace. Give him the chance to find who has dared to cross you in such an egregious way."

"Sven, did you not hear what just happened? I know you've always been hard-headed, but I never thought you to be stupid as well. He is no longer part of this family, why would I waste my resources helping him?"

"No resources, no help from us, all on his own. If he can bring proof of who is behind these attacks, I think maybe this small slight of bedding a woman no one wants could be forgiven ... with time?" Sven is talking faster than I've ever seen him.

Marko looks down at his plate before steepling his fingers in front of his face for a minute. The room is so quiet you could hear a pin drop.

"Josip, it truly pains me to let you go. You have two weeks, on your own to find me clear proof of who is behind this. If the evidence isn't conclusive, if I feel like one fact doesn't make sense, your death will not be swift. It will be an example for all, that even the smallest slights carry the biggest penalties. Leave me and do not return until the job is done."

He turns his head away from me, the end of the conversation. Sven comes over to me and takes everything I have in my pockets, my keys, my jewelry. Anything that I would have gotten while benefiting from my time with the Juric crime family and then he turns his back to me. I don't take it personally, as of right now I'm excommunicated. If he were to say one word to me it would be disrespectful. When I look towards Luka and Liam, they are in the same position, backs turned to the exile. I walk out of the room with nothing but my life to show for it.

I don't need any of that. All I need is the opportunity to make the bastards who hurt my girl pay, and that is exactly what these two weeks give me. Time and opportunity. Just enough time to kill them all.

11

Josip

The levity of the situation that I'm in hits me the second I walk outside and go to my car.

It's no longer my car. I have no keys. This car belongs to the Juric family along with my home and all my clothes. I literally have nothing but the clothes on my back.

I turn away from my car and start on the long journey ... the long journey nowhere. It's amazing how fucking cold the world seems when all you've ever known is miraculously taken away. I walk along the busy road that will lead me out of town making sure to keep my distance from the speeding cars.

A screeching sound of tires draws my attention.

"Josip?"

Keeley.

I look at her, but don't say a word as she probably doesn't know about her father removing me from the family.

"Did you hear me? What are you doing?" She speaks through the passenger side window, but I keep walking.

When the door opens and I hear her running up behind me I stop in my tracks. The last thing I want to do is alienate her. She has always been good to me. I'll let her know what is going on and then be on my way.

"Keeley, you can't talk to me." I tell her before she can get to a full stop in front of me.

"What, why in the hell not?" She crosses her arms over her chest and pops her hip out slightly, always full of attitude. I hear footsteps behind me and turn to see her husband Wire. His arms and hands full of scars from all his time in the Wings of Diablo MC. He is one of the deadliest enforcers I have ever had the pleasure of knowing and I know quite a few.

"Everything ok here?" He asks and I shake my head no.

"Neither one of you can talk to me."

"Yeah, you said that already. But you have yet to tell me why I shouldn't be talking to you? What is going on and why are you walking down the street?" Keeley leans her head to the side and waits for me to answer.

"Your father has removed me from the family. I'm exiled."

She gasps and put a hand to her mouth. She knows exactly what that means. "Impossible! Why the hell would he do something like that?"

"I want something that doesn't belong to me." I don't need to get into the details, but from the way her shoulders drop I know that she understands what I'm saying.

"You fell in love?"

"Yes."

"With whom?"

"Orabella De Luca."

"Orabella? I'm not familiar with her. I know Sloane and Leo." Keeley's eyes squint and she bites on the pad of her thumb trying to remember.

"You wouldn't, she has their name, but she's illegitimate and unwanted." I cringe at the thought.

"If they don't want her, why would that be a problem if you want to be with her?" Wire asks. He is deep into the motorcycle club world, but there is much about the Croatian mob that he has yet to understand.

"She bears the De Luca name, if they were to let me be with her, I could press for power in their family. Also, it's a form of punishment, her mother tricked Andrea into having her. She was a whore and just dropped Orabella off thinking that it would make Andrea take her into the family." I explain, but make sure to look around. The last thing I want is for someone to see me talking to them and they be punished for it.

89

"Fuck man, that's ridiculous. "

"I think so too, but that is the world that I live in. At least the world that I used to live in."

"Josip, I don't understand. I have never known of any exiled member of the family that wasn't either dead or sent off to some remote prison, left to rot and die. Sorry to sound cold, but what are you doing alive?" Keeley asks.

"Your father has given me two weeks to find out who is really behind all the kidnappings. If I can show him undeniable proof, he will entertain the idea of letting me return home. None of that is important though, he's giving me enough time to find Bella. That's all that I want to do. If they kill me after that, then so be it." I know that is the most realistic of all possibilities and truly I'm good with it. As long as Bella is out and safe, I don't care what the hell they do to me.

"Find Bella? Wait, she is one of the kidnapped women?" Wire asks and I nod my reply. "So why don't they just pay the-" His mouth turns into a small o, finally he gets it. "She's unwanted so paying the ransom for her is not high on their priority list."

"Exactly. They would rather her be tortured and killed then give in to their enemies." I clench my fists and look away as my anger tries to force its way back up.

"That's bullshit. Actually, it's typical. I can't stand that they did this to you for some unspoken fucking rule. I hate this." Keeley vents before she puts her hand out to me.

I look down at it then back at her, confused as to what she's doing.

"Come on, you're going to come with us."

I shake my head and turn to Wire. "No, I can't, if they even see me talking to you the both of you could get into some serious fucking trouble. No."

"What trouble? How can he tell me who I'm to talk to?" Keeley replies.

My eyes whip back towards her, "You are his daughter are you not? The entire Juric family must shun me. You know this, Keeley."

"I'm a married woman, if anyone has a claim on me it's Dillon. Father has already given him his blessing. I'm part of a whole new family now."

That was true, but I didn't think Marko would care about the semantics of it. One thing I do know is that he would never hurt his own daughter. If there is anyone I know who would be immune from the sadistic killer that is Marko Juric, it's Keeley.

"Yeah, come on. We got you." Wire walks back to the truck and Keeley grabs my arm tugging me behind.

"Where were you walking to?" He asks once I'm settled.

"I don't know. I have nothing. The minute Marko turned his back on me everything that I received while working for him was taken away. I have nothing but what you see."

"Fuck, you are going to need more than just a little bit of help. You're going to need a fucking miracle to get this shit done." He turns and drives back into traffic.

I sit in the back seat of the truck and watch as the desert whizzes by. I don't need a miracle, I'd just need to find a few more friends.

* * *

Keeley and Wire set me up with a room at the hotel they are staying at. They no longer live in Vegas so Wire doesn't have a great stash of money, but he gives me the three thousand dollars in cash he has on his person. Apparently, he had a good day at one of the craps tables on the strip. I get a burner phone and a few items of clothing—a pack of underwear, two pairs of pants and a pack of t-shirts. My entire wardrobe for the rest of my life costs me all of 40 bucks. They offer to stay around until I figure out some sort of plan and Wire tells me he'd use all the resources he has to assist me. It's nice to have friends in high places. He may no longer hold the title President of the original chapter of the Wings of Diablo, but he is the President of the nomad chapter. He only needs to call in a few favors and he would give me everything that he possibly can.

"What I need right now is a computer." Luckily, Keeley had packed one.

"Here it is. Keep it if you need to." She hands me her MacBook and the charger.

"I'll need it for at least the two weeks." I take the electronics from her.

"Josip, could I ask you a question? Personal?"

"Of course."

"If you knew she was off limits, why did you keep pursuing her? I know you are in love with her now, but I'm sure that took time."

I close my eyes and think back on when I had first met Bella. "I didn't know she was off limits until a few weeks after we met. But even if I had, I still would have wanted her. She's peace and purity. She's genuine. She's cares just because she can. Even though she's lived a life alone, she was quick to open up to me and it was almost involuntary that I opened up to her. I've never felt like I could truly just fucking be me with anyone. I couldn't give that up. I won't."

She smiles at me and reaches around to give me a hug. This is the second time in less than a week someone has just hugged me. It feels weird.

"I understand. We'll leave you to work. Let me know if you need anything."

"Thank you. I will never forget this." I pull away from her and walk over to the table in the hotel room and both of them leave. I get started with the most intense research I have ever done.

I go straight to the dark web to see if there is any more chatter about the ransoms. I didn't really know much about maneuvering around this platform, for the longest time Sven is the one I went to for this kind of information. I can't do that now.

There is a forum that is used by crime lovers, a really morbid place. There are times I would be able to get information from that, today is not one of those days.

"Sranje!" I slam my hand down on the table, frustration causing my chest to tighten. I'm getting nowhere with this. All I need is a starting point, but right now I don't seem to be getting any traction.

I could try one more avenue, but without loyalty to the family, I am hesitant to even make the attempt.

I pick up the burner phone that I'd bought earlier and call Kaja. Maybe word hasn't gotten down the lines yet.

He's my last link right now, I hope.

"*Da?*"

"Kaja, it's Josip." I wait for him to either hang up or curse me out.

"You're no longer part of the family." His voice is clear and my fucking gut drops. He knows. He's not going to be of any help. "Where are you?"

I stop my fingers from disconnecting the call. "What?"

"I can get away for a bit, but not for long. Sven told me about the deal. You can't do this on your own." Kaja speaks quickly through the phone.

"What about Marko disowning me?"

"As of right now, I like to think you're on probation. I'll help as much as I can without getting us both caught. Where are you?"

I quickly tell him the hotel and room number, and he's on his way.

I pace back and forth as I wait for him. I'm painfully aware of every second that passes. What the fuck happens when they realize that the De Lucas don't intend to give them whatever they want. Will they just kill Bella? Are they fucking hurting her right now?

I dig my hand in my hair and tug hard. I groan as my mind plays image after image of what they might be doing to her. Fucking bastards.

Fifteen minutes is all it takes for Kaja to get to the hotel, but it's more than enough time for me to go crazy with fucking anxiety.

I nearly rip the door off the hinges when he knocks.

"Josip, Hell. You need to get some rest." He walks by me into the room, but doesn't take his eyes off me.

"Rest? Are you fucking crazy? I don't have time for rest. I need to get fucking moving. I don't have time for this shit. None." I close the door and quickly walk back to where I was doing a piss poor job at research.

"How did the ransoms come in?"

"Messenger." Kaja answers immediately and he sits down next to me, taking the laptop in the process, and opening a few different pages that I had no clue about.

"What do you mean messenger? Like someone hand delivered the ransoms?"

"Exactly, they did it through various private mail carrier companies. They made it so each and every envelope would get to us at the same time, but the return addresses are all bogus."

I watch his fingers fly across the keyboard as he clicks and dismisses everything he comes across. "Did they leave a phone number? An account number?"

He turns in my direction for a second, "Wait, what do you think the ransoms are?"

"Money, of course?"

"No, not even close. According to what I've heard, they were all requests to give up certain allegiances or business opportunities. Whoever they are doesn't want money, they want us to give up our power, break promises and contracts, be seen as weak." Kaja turns back to the computer and continues what he was doing.

Fuck, Bella never had a chance, there is no way that they would give up any amount of power for her. She shouldn't even be there.

"I need to figure out who stands to gain from this. I need to figure out who is stupid enough to believe that this shit would work." I get up from the table and start pacing again. While Kaja is working there is nothing that I can do besides concoct new and exciting ways to kill whoever has Bella.

"So far there is no chatter about the ransoms, but there is one poster who seems to be just ahead of the curve. They could just be really good at getting information or they could know it firsthand. I can get an IP address, but it'll take a while."

"Do it. What about the photos from the Sever disappearance? Did they ever ID who it was?"

Kaja pulls up the photo on the other side of the screen, this time there are two other photos just as gritty of different angles, none of which show his face, just his hair and a piece of his side profile. "Nothing on these two. The cameras on the back of the property were disabled so we think they probably got out by foot. It's the only way."

I stare at the photo, but I can't place the man either. It's like a needle in a haystack to figure out who this is.

A knock on the door startles me out of my concentration. "*Da!*" I yell out.

"It's Wire. I brought you some things."

I walk over and open the door for him, but don't bother finding out what it is that he has. Instead, I rush back over to where Kaja is, not wanting to miss a second after he finds out who the poser is.

Wire walks in the room, but stops short when he sees Kaja.

"He's fine Wire. This is Kaja, a vor with the family."

When I see Wire's eyes squint, I realize he may not understand that term. "He's a made man. Trusted."

"I thought you said everyone in the family had to turn their back on you?"

"Kaja here decided today is the day to break the rules."

"No, didn't break them, just bending them a little." He nods in Wire's direction before continuing to type away.

"Josip, you don't need to be walking around without protection. Especially once Keeley and I go back home. I don't think this shit is going to be easy." Wire walks around me where the small dresser is and pulls up his shirt.

"I don't care if it's not easy. It needs to be fucking done." I look to see what he is doing.

"These will help." Wire pulls out three guns from the waist of his pants, a small vial of liquid, two knives, and some more cash.

"Fucking hell, where did you get this?" I walk over and pick up the vial to examine its contents—chloroform. This would definitely come in handy.

"I called a friend." He shrugs, fixes his shirt, and starts to walk away. "Keeley and I are going to get something to eat. Do you want something?"

"No."

"Josip, you have to fucking eat. Right now, you look like a stiff wind is going to blow you the hell over." Wire argues. "I'm all for handling business, but what fucking good are you going to be if you-" He looks over my shoulder at the computer. "What the fuck?"

I turn, but Kaja is still typing away trying to find information. "What?"

"You can't be fucking serious." Wire squints his eyes and moves me out of the way so he can look at the computer. Kaja stops typing and moves out of Wire's way as well. He is so close to the screen his fucking breath's going to fog up the screen.

"Is there a fucking problem?" Kaja asks.

"Yeah, there's a fucking problem. Where did you get this photo?"

I step closer to Wire, "You know who this is?"

"Yeah. We've been looking for this piece of shit for months."

My heartbeat picks up speed, "Who is it?"

"That's Rooster, the ex-President of the Spawns of Chaos MC."

12

Bella

"No, get off of me!" I yell as one of the bastard security guards pulls me into a room I only know as Hell.

The same group of people are there like always just waiting for me. A tall, light-skinned man with one entire eye and ear missing, a dark-skinned woman with dark blonde hair cut into an uneven bob, and finally a man with red hair the tips of it bleached slightly to give it an orange tinge. He's the same man that took me from the house.

"I don't know why you are making this so difficult for yourself. You know that it's only a matter of time before your people come for you, all you have to do is stay alive long enough. Cooperate." The man with the red hair speaks and I just stare at him. I couldn't cooperate, I don't know the answers to any of the questions that he keeps asking. It had only been a few days since I've been taken, but each day is worse than the last.

"Rooster, I think she may need a bit of encouragement." the woman says with a sinister smirk on her face.

"Muñeca, I really hate to do this to you, but you need to learn what battles to fight and when you should just give up. Now, are you going to tell me about the October deal and Leo De Luca."

I blow out a deep breath, "How many times do I have to tell you I don't know anything. He is only my half-brother and I don't have the privilege of knowing about anything that is happening with the family."

I'd told them all the same thing over and over, but either they didn't believe me or they just enjoy hearing me scream.

"Put her in the tub." Rooster says and the two guards that dragged me out of the room pull me to a large basin-like tub. It looks to be made of a heavy wood. From the outside it is just like a regular tub, but once I get a glimpse at the inside, I see two large metal hoops jutting out from the bottom. They put me inside latching my wrist and ankle cuffs to one of the hoops so I'm sitting with my knees up to my chest and my arms between my legs.

"Are you sure there is nothing that you want to tell

me? What about the guards I asked you about yesterday?"

"I don't know anything." I repeat.

"Camy, a little assistance?" Rooster calls to the woman who claps her hands once and rushes over to where I am. She takes a length of rope from one of the guards and stands behind me.

I cringe in surprise when I feel her pulling my hair out of the ponytail it's been in since I'd gotten here. "What are you doing?"

"Shut the fuck up! You don't want to help us, that means you don't have any reason to be talking." Rooster screams at me.

I feel Camy wrap the rope around my hair like a scrunchie before she begins to braid my hair with the rope entwined in the strands. I don't understand what she is doing until she jerks my head all the way back, stretching my neck as far as it will go and she fastens the rope to the hoop behind me.

In this position not only is it hard to breath, but my back is arched as far as it will go and my hair is pulled to the point of almost ripping out of my scalp. I can only move my head slightly from side to side to get any relief.

I jump when a loud noise followed by the rush of water erupts from behind me.

"What the ... hell ... is this." I can barely talk with my head in this position. I lean my head to the side slightly and can see the water is rapidly filling the tub already up to my calves.

"Please. I don't know anything. I'm worthless to them."

"You are their family, you share their last name, you live in their house. You can't be worthless no matter what you try to get me to believe." Rooster says as he slowly walks back around to the man with the missing eye and ear. They are both on the side of me, I can see them out of the corner of my eye. I've never heard him speak, but I know he can. Every so often Rooster will lean in and the man will whisper something in his ear—an order.

Rooster might be the one with the mouth, but it's the man with one eye that holds the power.

The water rises up to my chest and I start to pull at my restraints. My mouth is dry, because I'm hyperventilating. I pull at the restraint in my hair not caring if I ripped every strand of hair I had off, but the braid and the rope make it impossible. I feel burning on certain portions of my scalp where I have ripped my hair out, but it isn't enough to get free.

As the water makes its way to my chest the panic really begins to sink in. I scream and beg for them to show mercy on me. I cry and curse everyone in my life, starting with my gold digging mother for forcing me on Andrea. Then Andrea for not looking past the fact that I am an illegitimate child.

"Tell me about the October deal." I hear Rooster say.

"Oh God! I don't know! I swear it! I don't know! Please. Please!" My entire body shakes in fear as I kick and pull at my restraints willing a bone to break or hunk of flesh to tear off so I can get free. I feel the burn as the restraints cut into my ankles and wrists, but it's nothing compared to the burn in my chest as my heart palpitates faster than I have ever felt it and my ribs struggle to expand in the position that I'm in. The water gets up to my neck and back of my head.

"No ... Help me! Ahh!" I scream and with the last bits of strength I have, I yank on my arms. I feel a hard pull and a dull pop only. "Ahhh!" I wail in intense pain as my arm has dislocated from my shoulder.

The water covers my ears and I can no longer hear what's going on in the room. I say my final prayers as the water makes its way to my hairline and starts to cover my eyes. Something moves behind me and just as suddenly as it started the stream of water stops, leaving only my eyes, mouth and nose out of the liquid.

I cry in pain, in relief, and in fear. I just cry.

The spasms in my back are so painful after a few moments of being stuck in this position it feels like the bones are breaking.

I open my mouth to call out, but the second I do a stream of water rushes in. I cough and try to spit it out, but with every movement my face is covered with the water. I force myself to stay still and swallow whatever is in my mouth, to cough as best I can in this position and still keep my airway open.

"Please don't leave me. Don't leave me." I say as loud as I can, but it's too late. From my peripheral vision, I see the door open and the three of them walk out. Without even giving me a second glance.

* * *

I PASS out three times in that position, but each time I wake back up as I'm drowning. It feels like they'd kept me here for hours. The only thing that I can do is stay awake and keep my head in this position. It is the only way for me to survive.

The door is pushed open, Camy and Rooster stroll back in. I'm so exhausted I can't even beg them to have mercy on me. I've never been one to contemplate suicide, but I am ready to just turn my head to the side and drown. I am worthless anyway.

"Would you look at my little fish? That is such a pretty position for you." Rooster leans over me. "Fine, if you want to keep your secrets to yourself, I guess I can't force them out. Maybe tomorrow you'll want to help me." He pulls out a long knife and presses it to my face. I don't flinch. I want him to do it, to just end this.

He reaches his arm into the tub with me and cuts the rope that ties my head to the loop. The sudden release causes my body to list to the side. Since my hands and legs are still tied down, my head just goes further under the water. I have no energy to right myself and even as my lungs begin to seize from all the water I'm sucking down, it still feels better than being in that position.

Rooster takes his time to reach in and unlatch my hands from the front loop followed by my ankles. He lifts me up out the tub and drops me on the hard floor. I vomit foamy water and cough all the while trying to suck in a much needed breath. I stretch out my legs and one arm that is functional. The pain of trying to use my limbs after being stuck in that position is excruciating.

"Take her back to the room, bring the Bianucci woman out."

The guards drag me out of Hell and back into the room with the rest of the prisoners. I scream as they have no sympathy for my injured arm or the torment that I was just put through. All they care about is getting the next one on the list. That is all this is, a constant repeating torture session.

I do my best to stand when we get to the room that I've been forced to stay in, but my feet don't want to work for me. I try again, because I know if they drag me, it'll be that much worse. The floor is rotted wood, a constant source of scraps and splinters. There are eleven women here, there used to be twelve, but one was killed about three days ago. Her body is still laying in the middle of the floor, bloating and bringing flies. The stench curls the hairs on the inside of my nose. The eleven of us are all lined up on one wall chained at the ankle by a short length of chain. I've only been here for a few days, but some of the other women have been here for weeks. Even though we are all together, the ones that have been here the longest have become almost feral. The constant torture, the pain and maybe worst of all the starvation is taking its toll. They don't feed us. They bring down one bottle of water about thirty two ounces that we are supposed to share between all of us. They don't wash us, and there is only a bucket that we must past down the line when someone has to relieve themselves. There is one woman here who had her menstruation cycle, with no feminine products she bled through her clothing and down her legs. The dried blood is still caked on her. She has it the worst when we are able to sleep. The bugs bite and crawl on her the most. The same bugs being the only thing some of the women have eaten since the beginning.

On one occasion when Rooster came in, one of the women had asked him when he was going to feed us. He beat her to death in front of us, the same woman that's now rotting on the floor. I remember realizing just how crazy he was when he told us if we were that hungry, she was all the food we needed. He intended for us to eat the dead woman's flesh. I haven't even looked in that direction, but I've caught some of the women who have been here longer staring at that putrid flesh like it's Sunday dinner.

"Your arm?"

Katarina Juric, the woman to the left of me and the only one I've spoken with since I've been here speaks up. Her voice croaks with each word.

I suck in breaths through my clenched teeth. The pain in my arm pulses with each heartbeat.

"We have to put that back in place." She turns to me, her movements are slow. Her lips are so cracked that with every word her lips bleed.

"I can't, I don't want to move." I grunt out.

"The longer you leave it, the harder it is going to be." She does her best to sit up.

"No, I can't" I know what she has to do, but I just don't think I could handle the pain.

"The pain will go away once its back in place." Katarina shakes her head and blinks a few times, probably to get the fog out of her brain.

I try to move the lame arm, but nothing happens, just more searing pain.

"Ok, let's do it." I turn all the way around so my face is to the wall and my injured arm is near her. I lean my head against the slick rock and let her position my arm. I scream in agony. A few of the girls cry while others tell me to shut the hell up and die already. My body shakes and my skin feels cold. I'm sure I would be sweating if I weren't already so dehydrated.

After five tries, Katarina is finally able to get my arm back in place. She was right, the pain decreases dramatically when it is back in the socket. But just as the pain in my arm begins to decrease, the pain in my head rises to barely tolerable levels. I touch my neck and there is sticky blood coming from my head. With my hand I touch my head and sure enough there are several places I'd ripped my scalp off. In some places large chunks were pulled off and other places have small gashes in the skin where it split.

"I'm sorry I can't do anything about that." Katarina looks at my head.

"That's ok. I just have to remember not to put my head down on the floor." I try to joke about it, but I start to think about the random bugs crawling up my skin to get to the open wounds in my head. I use my good arm to lift my long hair up and wrap it up as best I could into a top knot. Times like this I regret keeping my hair this long.

"I told them." Katarina sits back against the wall.

"What?"

"I told them everything they wanted to know. I betrayed my family." Her eyes squeeze shut, but there are no tears.

"Of course, you told them, your family will know you had no choice." I do my best to console her.

"You really don't know my father, do you?" She

scoffs and turns back to me. Her bright gold eyes the only thing on her face that show a bit of life.

"No, unfortunately, I've never had the pleasure."

"The pleasure. Meeting him would have been no pleasure. I spent years trying to prove to my father that I'm good enough. I didn't grow up with him, but he always made his presence known. I looked up to him. Idolized him. Only to find out that I would never be good enough, because I have a fucking vagina between my legs. It took him years before he let me become a bratok. It's the highest station I will ever hold. When he finds out that I snitched, either he'll kill me or he'll make me step down. I'm kind of hoping it's the former."

"Don't talk like that. It'll work out. Everything will work out." I rub her arm and pull her in for a hug. Her body shudders as waterless tears rack her frame. When she pulls back, her lips find mine in an intimate kiss. It takes a second for my brain to figure out what is going on. I pull away abruptly.

"Katarina no!" I hiss at her.

"Hmm, sorry. I couldn't help myself. When you told me, you weren't married I thought maybe there was a chance."

"I'm not married, but I'm taken. Sort of." I sigh and desperately try to remember what Josip sounds like. For some reason, I am having a hard time remembering the exact tone and normal cadence of his voice. I can see him in my dreams and memories, but I can't hear him right anymore. It's painful.

"Sort of? How can you sort of be taken?"

"Well, it's complicated." I say not wanting to bore her with my long story.

She shakes the chain attached to her leg. "Does it look like I'm going anywhere any time soon?"

I stop to think about the fact that it's someone in her family, she may get upset or even find a way to get him punished. I don't want that, but I want to speak his name to someone. Let someone know how much I love him.

"I don't want to get anyone in trouble, it's one of your people." I don't look at her, but I feel her body move when she turns in my direction.

"One of my people? They are part of the Juric Family?"

I nod.

"By name or by honor?"

"Honor."

"How about this, whatever we talk about in this fucked up place will stay here. I won't address it if we ever get out, besides my father will be through with me before I'd be able to say anything." When I look up at her she animatedly wiggles her eyebrows making me laugh. "So, who is it?"

I close my eyes and savor the feel of his name on my tongue, "Josip."

"Jebote!" Katarina says loudly. "Holy shit, are you serious? I would have never in a million years guessed that. He's such a cold fish. Very prim and posh. Josip? Really?"

"He's not. Not the real Josip. When he no longer has to put on a facade for the people around him, Josip is warm. He's caring and attentive. Possessive. He's perfect." Those words don't do him justice, but it's all I have right now.

"Why have I never seen you then? Is this new between you two?"

"No. It's been going on for years, but remember when I told you about being illegitimate and how my family basically sees me as a black spot on their perfect family tree?"

"Yeah."

"Well, it also means that I'm forbidden to marry or be with anyone, especially someone with ties to a different family. They don't want my husband trying to push his way into a power spot. They don't want my seed to be the one to carry on the De Luca name. I'm the mistake they just want to wash away." I sigh and my head pounds harder with the motion. "Josip and I have been having a secret relationship for two years."

"Wow ... that's just ... wow." Katarina leans back against the wall, her eyebrows still raised and a pensive look on her face. "You know he won't be able to come for you right?"

"I know."

I'm never going to get out of here, not alive. My family isn't going to come for me or pay for me, Josip will not be allowed to either. I look over to the door we were all brought in and fantasize about seeing him walk in. Fantasies are all I will ever have.

13

Josip

Figuring out that the man in the photo is Rooster is only a piece of the puzzle, but not the first step. According to Wire, Rooster had done something like this before with an enemy of his club. Duo, Liam Juric's daughter, is the one he had helped kidnap. Now it seems he has a taste for it. We still don't know where Rooster is, what we do know is where Mr. Finn Montgomery works. Finn is the dark web poster with all the information.

Once Kaja is able to get me a name and an address I am able to really get moving. I find out where he works, his wife and children's names, where his mother is buried, followed by all his debts and secrets he'd want to keep hidden. Including the fact that he had a nasty habit of meeting up with underage teenagers.

That is my in. I lure him out with promises of a date with a 16 year old high school track star. It's surprising how easy it is for me to get him to agree, a few stock photos from the internet and a promise of something more is enough for him to agree to meet up. When I have Keeley call him, it is a done deal.

The only issue is he lives in Colorado so I have to get there. Wire's able to set something up with one of his Wings of Diablo brothers, Fly. Apparently, he is a pilot with quite a few connections. I have a private flight just three hours after saying I needed one.

Kaja has to stay near the family in case he's called on, but the three of them promise that if I need help with anything that all I have to do is call. Wire offers to come along with me, but I can't risk it getting back to Marko and him doing something to Keeley as punishment. I don't think he will hurt her, but there are other things that can be done to make her regret helping me.

I take the money they are able to spare, my photo of Rooster, and the address of the man I will get my first round of answers from.

* * *

THE MAN AGREES to meet up in two days. I spend the next day shopping for things that I will need to get him to talk. I'm almost giddy with excitement at the thought of being the one to get him to talk. I've been around countless torture sessions, stood by while others maimed and killed. I know the worst and slowest of ways for someone to die. I plan to make sure Finn tells me everything he knows before I end his useless life.

The difference between everyone else in the family and me is now I have no leash. There are no boundaries I can't cross, no rules I have to follow, nothing but my own satisfaction.

I reach out to Kaja every day to see if there has been any updates. So far, most all of the families have begun giving in to the ransom demands. But no hostages were returned as of yet. No Bella.

Every day I know she is still missing, the demon in me grows more and more hungry for death and blood.

The house that I instruct Finn to come to is a bit secluded and near one of the old shutdown skiing trails. There's no snow right now, so no tourists that may accidentally stumble in my direction. The house actually is a safe house for the Wings of Diablo club and I have full use of it.

I set up the inside just like I had told that piece of shit Finn I would—rose petals and candles. When I hear the car pull up, I set the prop female cut out I got from the party supply store. Nothing like a visual to get him to let his guard down. The door to his car slams and I can hear him bound up the stairs. On the door in pretty, girly handwriting is a note that tells him to come in, that the doorbell isn't working properly.

The nasty, scrawny looking man walks in without checking his surroundings.

"Katie? You upstairs sweet girl?" He has a small plastic bag in his hand with what looks to be generic wine. He's about four inches shorter than me and I can see dandruff on his dark sweater. I hide in the shadows a while longer until he is fully inside the house. I ready the rag in my hand and wait for my opening. "Katie, I'm c-" His words are cut off when I press the rag with chloroform against his mouth and nose. He struggles for a few seconds before he drops down to the floor unconscious.

Now let the pain begin.

14

JF

Josip

"What the hell ... what is this? Help! Help me someone! Please! Oh God please help me!" Finn screams out when he finally wakes up.

"*Šuti!*" I bark at him and walk over so he can see me. "Keep your mouth shut unless I give you permission to talk. If you don't, things are going to go from bad to fucked up far quicker than I'd like."

"Who ... who are you? What do you want?"

I pull my hand back and punch him directly in the face. He has to spit the blood up since he can't turn his head. I have him stripped and tied down to a long wooden table that looks to be used for picnics.

"Did you not hear me tell you to keep your mouth shut?" I grab hold of his hair and when he finally is able to open his eyes, he nods his head yes. "Good, now Finn, you did something bad. I'm just here to get some answers from you. Do you know who I am? You may speak when I ask you a question." I stand back and wait for him to speak.

"Katie's father, look, I wasn't going to do anything ... I was just going to talk to her."

"Finn, stop fucking lying. I already know about your sick and twisted obsession with little girls. I should kill you for that alone, pieces of shit like you make me happy I don't have any children. Katie isn't real. I needed to get you here and that ruse was the easiest way. I want you to answer some questions about what is going on with all the kidnappings ... Juric Family, Sever Family, Vavra family, Bianucci Family?" With every name I say his eyes get wider and wider.

"Kidnappings? I don't know anything about kidnappings." I grab a tool off the side table and quickly walk over to him. Pulling the gag down by his neck back up to his mouth and get to work.

A hand drill with high RPM and torque is wonderful for pushing through skin. I made sure to get a high voltage wired one so I didn't lose any power. They are compact, and no one questions someone in a hardware store picking up a new drill.

I place the drill bit in the center of his kneecap and hold down the power. I can barely hear his screams over the grind and whirr of the powerful machine. Thankfully, I picked up some goggles on the recommendation of the salesclerk, 'safety first' she had said. The blood and small specks of bone fly up onto my face as I press into his leg with all my might. The diamond-tipped drill bit gets through the bone and into the soft tissue before crunching its way through the joint and finally exiting the other side of his leg.

My face and chest are covered in his blood and even though he is still wailing, it's not enough. This bastard helped get my Bella taken. How fucking dare he lay here and tell me he doesn't know who they are.

I quickly go over to his other side and repeat the process on that leg. By the time I finish, the floor is slick with his blood and I have to use some of the rope to create tourniquets so he doesn't bleed out.

I walk up to the top of the table where Finn is convulsing and whimpering in pain. His screaming stopped about halfway through the second knee.

"Now, I'm going to ask you again and if you give me an answer I don't think is truthful, I'm going to take the drill and poke many more holes into you. You understand?"

He nods his head slowly.

"Good." I pull the gag down, "What do you know about it?"

"I'm just an Interpol worker. I didn't know anything like this was going to happen. I'm sorry. I'm sorry. Please ... Don't hurt me anymore. Please." His begging is pitiful and I almost smack him again just to get him to shut up.

"Are you saying you didn't have anything to do with it?"

"No. I didn't." He answers, but he hesitates first. Liars get the drill.

I pull the gag up to his mouth and he screams for me to wait even before I am able to pick the drill up again. I will not wait. I don't have time for mercy. I need straight answers, right now.

I put four new holes in Finn's body. One in each hand and one in each shoulder, then I use the wax from the candles I've been burning to pour in each of these open wounds. Better to switch things up. The wax acts as a cauterizing agent of sorts, not the best, but it'll do for now. This time he passes out and I have to wake him up before I could finish.

Once everything is situated again, I pull the gag off and wait for him to calm down a bit.

"You're not losing that much blood. This could go on for a long time." I wipe off my goggles and wait for him to start talking again.

"I know who the marks are, but I never found out exactly who is behind it. I swear it to you. They told me if I helped them, they would pay me five million a year for the rest of my life and make sure I never went to jail for ... my illness." A scowl turns up my face, he's a fucking pedophile, I'm going to take pity on him.

"What did they have you do?"

"It was a long project, going on for almost a year. They gave me a list of names and I needed to find each time they flew out of country or purchased any means of travel. Automobile records. Then they gave me names of people associated with all that information. By the end of it all there was at least three boxes worth of information." He sucks in a deep breath and continues. "Once they were gone, I didn't hear anything. No money, no immunity, they'd conned me. So, I looked up the information including the travel history of the man I'd been in contact with. It was only then that everything began clicking together. Photos of some of the women they had me looking for being hauled onto trains and private planes."

"I want the name of your contact and all the information you found."

"I don't have it ... it's at work." He shakes his head.

"*Lažljivac!*" I don't even bother with the gag, instead I take the drill and stick it in his eye. It only takes a second for the bit to catch and rip the squishy globe out of his face. "Stop fucking lying to me!"

I know for sure he didn't leave it at work, he probably didn't even look it up on his work computer. All those government computers are monitored. Even if he did find all the information at work, he surely wouldn't store it there. The information is somewhere only he would know and access. I'd put money on it, if he had a copy saved in the cloud.

His teeth chatter and his one good eye rolls in his head.

"Tell me where I can find it or I start making soup out of your intestines."

"Saved. Online."

I fucking knew it.

I rush to my bag and pull out my laptop. I use the man's clothes to wipe my hands before I open it up and set up where he can see. It's a difficult process, but he walks me through all the firewalls and backdoors until I get to the information he'd saved on the server. I open it up first and it's almost 10 gigabytes of scanned documents and photos, video clips, and numbers. Along with the information on a small team that specialized in abductions. I don't know them to be part of any family, but I will find out. I save it all to my personal cloud using an encryption password so it will be harder to get into.

"Let me go. Nothing else. Please." Finn moans weakly from the table. There is no way that I will be able to do that. He's already seen my face and he knows that I'm looking for these people. He's a liability, besides there are other sins that he needs to atone for.

"Good job, now that I've got all that out of the way, let's talk about what you were going to do with Katie." I grab for my drill as he weeps in defeat.

By the end of the night, I had made Finn's urethra a lot wider, his balls a lot smaller and his ability to scream for help a lot harder. I kill him by drilling holes into his lungs and watch him suffocate on his own blood.

I'm exhausted after that. I don't know how people did this all day and are still able to walk around like nothing happened. All I want is a drink and a nap.

I let Wire know that I'd be finished with the house tomorrow and that there's a present for his cleaner buddies to take care of. Then I strip out of my clothes, take a shower, and go to sleep. I'm feeling a little more at peace than I have been in the past few days and one step closer to getting my Bella back.

15

JF

Josip

It takes another four days to find and get to the location of my next target. I went through the information that I got from Finn. I don't know about the other families, but for all the information on the Juric family he had I knew exactly what it was—shipping dates, meetings with associates and business partners. I only knew about these transactions, because I had attended each one of them. I made sure the deals were solid and upheld. Ensuring that every detail matched what was agreed on. Whoever is behind this had an ongoing list of all the business transactions that the families were a part of. They could pick and choose which ones they want them to give up. It's almost genius. Find out what the demand is for something then force whoever is supplying it to back down.

Wire has been a fucking godsend. I go through him and his people for travel and to find out who the team lead is. He continues to ask if I need him to ride up and help me, but I keep turning him away.

On my way to the peep show bar that my next target likes to visit, I get a call I'm not expecting.

"Da?"

"Josip, It's Kaja." He speaks and waits for my acknowledgement. He shouldn't be calling me. Something has happened.

"What's going on?" I lean against the wall, holding my breath until he starts to talk again.

"They've started releasing the hostages. Katarina made it back."

Oh God. "Bella?"

Kaja doesn't reply to my question "Katarina wants to talk to you."

"Kaja, no!" I try to tell him, but it's too late, he's already shifting the phone. Katarina is a bratok, higher than Kaja in the family and Marko's blood daughter. If there is anyone who is going to uphold the rules it's her.

"Josip, you there?"

"I'm exiled, you can't-"

She cuts me off before I can finish, "Fuck that. Fuck all that right now. Listen to me. You need to move faster."

I'd known Katarina for years and there has rarely been a woman I found to be more callous than her. I've never seen her cry. Though I can hear the emotion and cracking of her voice right now.

"Bella is still alive and she loves you. She's strong and fighting, but she won't last much longer. Tell me you're close to finding an answer!" Katarina sniffles and sucks in a ragged breath.

"Yes, I'm close. I think I'm close. I'm about to get one of the guards who was part of the team of kidnappers." I reply quickly.

"Good, we were all in one place. I don't know the location, but if he tells you where he dropped us off, you'll find Bella. Find her and bring her home."

I put my free hand in my hair and pull. I knew that time was running out, but to hear Katarina say this is like an exclamation point on the ticking clock. I'm so close, but she's right I have to move faster. I have already gone through a week of the time that Marko has given me. I need to finish this now.

"I will."

"I don't want to believe that you will, I told her you wouldn't. Part of me believes she knows you will." Katarina wishes me luck and then turns the phone back over to Kaja.

"Where are you?"

"Chicago."

"What the hell are you doing all the way over there?"

"It's where Doberman is." I look to the entrance of the sleezy bar and watch the people walking in and out.

"Doberman? I've never heard of him."

"Yeah, me neither. But he's about to hear of me." I growl into the phone and Kaja actually has the nerve to chuckle.

"What the fuck is funny?" I bark at him.

"Josip, I've never even seen you kill a fucking bug, yet here you are plotting killing and torturing motherfuckers. It's a good look for you."

"You know what they say, it's the quiet ones you have to watch out for. I'll let you know when I have any further information. Thanks, Kaja."

I hang up before he can say anything else. I walk over to the club and Doberman is the first bastard I see. He's tall and built, with a ponytail and is balding slightly at the top.

I stay there and watch the girls dance, drinking the right amount of alcohol to make it look like I'm not specifically waiting for him. He stays there for a few hours and by the time he is ready to leave he is stumbling around.

I wait a few seconds so it doesn't seem like I am leaving after him and then I walk out. I do my best to make it seem as if I'm just as drunk as everyone else leaving the club, but in reality, I've only had one drink. I've been leaving all the other drinks around the bar.

I find Doberman behind the bar near his car pissing like a fucking jerk on the side of the wall. Nasty fuck. I sneak up behind him, wait for him to put his dick back in his pants and inject him in the neck with a sedative. It's not instantaneous and he turns to fight me.

"Motherfucker, what the hell is this?" his words slur from both the medication and the booze.

"Your reckoning I suspect."

"Fuck you, boyo!" He swings a heavy arm in my direction. The man has at least three inches of arm length on me. If I am going to fight him, I will have to get as close to him as possible. Not something I really want to do, but he's not really giving me a choice. I slide under his punch and take a step into his space. I hit him two times in the side and use my elbow to hit him once in the chin. I'm not the biggest man so on a regular day when he is sober my blows probably wouldn't do much to slow him down. Except today when he is this drunk, he stumbles and it's all I need to take him out. I pepper his face with punches until the last one along with the drug I'd injected him with is enough to knock him out cold. I leave him there by the wall and his car rushing to get my rental.

Not one person has walked by and I look around the area to see if there are any surveillance cameras. That's the great thing about these dirty places. No one ever wants to get caught coming out of one.

* * *

THE NEXT TIME Doberman wakes up he is tied to a concrete column with a special collar around his neck. I thought it funny that he would name himself after a dog only to be killed by a collar.

"What the fuck do you want?" His voice slurs and he swings his head from side to side trying to find me. It's cold in Chicago, I had to build a small fire to keep warm while I waited for him to wake up. I rub my hands together one more time before I make my way over to him.

"I'll fucking kill you. You have no idea who the fuck you are messing with! I've killed men three times your size. You piece of shit!" He yells at me.

I wait impatiently for him to stop his rant.

"Doberman, do you know who I am?"

"Yeah, a fucking dead man." He growls.

"No, that'll be you shortly." I give him a polite smile and take another step closer to him. "Doberman, I'm not a man who has a lot of time or anything to lose. You on the other hand have everything to lose. Your rank, your money, your life."

He laughs exaggeratedly, "Do you think I care if I fucking die? I don't! I've been waiting for death for a decade."

"Is that so? Let me help you out with that then." I flick a switch on the crude bomb I've attached to his neck, a countdown of twelve minutes starts.

"What is this? What are you doing?" The bravado that was lacing his voice seconds ago gone and fear takes its place.

"You have twelve minutes to tell me every detail about the kidnappings. The Juric family, Bianucci family, Vavra family all of them. If you don't this small device will blow your head clear off your body." He opens his mouth to speak, but I put my hand up to stop him. "Before you say anything about if I kill you that I won't get the information, remember that you have a whole team I can go through. I'll just kill each and every one of you until I get the answers I need."

"I don't know what you're talking about."

I look down at the clock, "eleven minutes."

"Look! Just get this thing off and I'll tell you everything I know."

"What is this going to do for you? Kao muha bez glave. What is stalling going to help you achieve?" I tilt my head to the side and just stare at the idiot.

"Okay, okay fine! Fuck! My team and I were contracted to sneak in and kidnap a list of people. We were all paid well, ten million each, we got half up front and the second half we get once the job was done."

"Let me guess, no one came through with the second half?"

"No, the motherfuckers conned us. We planned and delivered all those women only to be given the shit end of the stick."

I pull a photo of Rooster out of my pocket. "Is this the man that you were working for?"

"That's one of them. Rooster. At least that is what he said his name was. The crazy motherfucker. He insisted that we let him come on the missions with us. He made things interesting. There were two others that worked with him. A woman named Camy and a man whose name I never got. Rooster did all the talking, but it seemed like the other man was the one in charge of everything. He never fucking talked. Not once."

I look at the man's neck. Seven minutes left. "Seven minutes, you better start talking faster."

"Shit man what the fuck! I'm giving you everything. What the hell do you want to know?" He pulls at the restraints, but made sure he was tied up tightly. I don't have time to try and run him down if he manages to get away.

"Where did you drop them off? How many did you drop off?"

"Twelve, we dropped off twelve." He says quickly. "We tried to go back for the rest of our money, but the guards shot and killed two of my men before we could even open our mouths. Rooster told us if we ever showed our faces again that the punishment would be more severe. I'd take five million over death any day."

Five minutes left.

"Where is it?"

"Benton Harbor, Michigan. There is a small service road off Graham Avenue that leads you to Ox Creek. A few businesses are out there and a golf course, there is a large community development that they are using. It's all locked up, still under-construction. They took the girls in there. I don't know exactly which house! Now, come on, take this off!" He whines and the sweat pours down his face. There's a little under four minutes left.

I grab the collar, but instead of turning it off, I just make sure it's on secure. There is no way for me to turn it off, not that it was even an option.

"You took my woman and delivered her to those fucking monsters. Do you really think that I will let you go?"

"No, you can't ... wait! I can help you, get you inside. We can take them for all they're worth." He shakes and pulls, "Come on man please! Let me go!" He cries hard. I don't need him to get me in. I don't want to take them for all they're worth. I want to get my woman. He's not needed for that. I walk away from him quickly. The amount of explosives I'd used in the collar is more than enough to blow his head clear off his shoulders. We are in an abandoned construction site so even though I'm not concerned about waking the neighbors I will still have to do some cleaning up. It will give me just enough time to think about my next step. One way or another tomorrow will be the last day of all this shit. Tomorrow I'd have my Bella.

16

JF

Josip

The bastard had told the truth about everything that he divulged. There is indeed a small community of still in construction houses right by the river. The problem I have is I don't know which of these houses is the one that Bella might be in.

I spoke with Kaja this morning and he assured me that nothing had changed, no one called to tell them that Bella had been killed. He did tell me that new orders were passed down from Marko, since my two weeks was almost up. If I didn't hold up my side of the bargain, they would come to kill me. That's fine, I wasn't trying to run away from them. I am just trying to make sure my woman is safe first.

I stay back for a few minutes and just examine the

scene. There are a few cars, but I don't really see anyone driving or walking around for that matter. There is one car that I'm surprised to see here. It's a Maserati and from the looks of it in very good condition.

I need to move fast.

I let Wire know that this is the end of the road and I will need to get out of town fast and back to Las Vegas, so he has Fly set up a private flight for me. I only need to get to the private airstrip. I don't know if I'm going to have anyone chasing after me so I really hope that I can trust what he told me.

All of the houses look the same and Katarina couldn't really tell me anything besides there is a long hallway that leads to some stairs. The problem is none of the houses are completely built except for two and I'd already checked those.

I pull the hood of my sweater over my head and start moving forward. I check the first house that is still under construction and find that the groundwork isn't even properly laid. I move from there and hustle over to the next one. There is one guard laying on a semi-built deck with a cigarette in his mouth looking up at the night sky. Fuck him and his relaxation.

I pull out one of the knives from the sheath on my side and as quietly as I can sneak up behind him and slam the thin metal into the side of his head. His temple's just soft enough to not give me any resistance.

A small stream of blood dribbles out of the

wound as I yank my knife out of his skull. I check the man's pockets to see if he has anything of use. I find a cell phone, but it's password protected. I slip it into my pocket, someone else may be able to open it.

The next house over is a bit more built up, but none of the windows are in. I bend down and start to make my way over there, but a swarm of security guards come out the back of one of the houses running in my direction.

Fuck, they know I'm here.

I duck down as a car comes from the opposite direction and meets the men running from the other house in the center of the road. A woman gets out and they start talking. Whatever they are saying to each other seems a bit animated, but I can't really pick up on any of the words.

The woman gets back into the car and drives off to where the other cars are parked, while the guards all run in my direction. I need to get out of here before they catch me. There is no way that I'll be able to take them all on by myself.

I run over towards the house with no windows as the group of them run past the house I was in and take off for the fence. They must be working their way up from the back. I'll be able to lay low for a second or so in this house. Just as I get to the window a guard I didn't see comes walking around the corner. I lunge in his direction before he can see me and I grab his chin and the top of his head.

"What the fuc-"

I snap his neck before he can even get the full sentence out of his mouth or think to fight back. I make sure his body doesn't hit the ground, but instead drag it over to the side of the house where it might be harder for one of the other guards to see. I need to get out of sight and fast.

I hop into the window and just as I'm about to stand up something hard hits me on the side of my head. The blow is enough to stagger me, but I know if I fall that's it. I can't black out. I need to fight. The person swings the pipe again, but the swing is sloppy. I try to pull my knife back out, but my hand lands on the butt of my gun instead. In the same motion I grab hold of the pipe, pull out my gun and push the bastard against the wall.

I jam the gun up under their chin, but the person is much smaller than I would have anticipated. My heart breaks in two and then stitches back up better than before when I get a good look at who I'm holding.

"Oh ... fuck ... Bella?"

17

IF

Bella

Just when I thought life couldn't get any worse, it does.

These bastards were true to their word. Everyone who paid the ransoms got their people back. I'm not one of those people and know that I won't be. Though I am sure once they realize that I'm not going to get out the way they want me to Rooster and his friends will just kill me. That's not the case. As it stands right now there is only me and one other woman, Christine Bianucci left. The pain is now only split up between the two of us. Instead of killing me like I thought they would, I've become their personal toy.

"Get up!" Water from a large bucket splashes my face and I'm being pulled by my hair before I have a chance to even wake up.

"What! Let me go!" I scream and try to get my feet under me, but I'm moving too fast.

They strap me to a chair outside of the main room. A room that I've never been in. "What do you want?" I look around the room and see there is another two men besides Rooster and the man with the scars on his face. I don't know much about other families' business and who is who, but I would bet a lot of money that these two men are part of someone's mafia.

"I don't know her. Are you sure she is part of the De Luca family?" One of the men says with a very thick European accent.

"Yes, the pendejos didn't want to pay the ransom. I guess she's not an important member, but I'm sure there is still a demand for her."

"I'll ask Yemen. I doubt it though, why don't you just kill this one?"

"I'd hate for all that work to go to waste." Rooster shrugs. "Let me get the other one. Her family wasn't able to get the ransom paid in time, but they did make a strong effort."

The both of them walk out of the space leaving me with the second man that I don't know.

"You're a pretty little thing aren't you." The man walks up closer to me.

"I'm not a little thing." I snarl at him. My voice is weak, but I stare daggers at him.

"Oh, no, don't be mean." He reaches out and tries to

stroke my hair. I pull my head away and his hand misses its mark.

"Don't you fucking touch me!" I yell at him the best that I can.

He grabs my face and snatches a hand into my hair. I scream in agony as my scalp isn't healed and him pulling on my hair only reopens the small scabs that have started to form.

"You must not understand what the fuck is going on here. We are here to figure out what Ilia will do with you. You're worthless right now. I could have you for myself if I asked. You'll learn to please me. You'll be begging for my cock before too long. Be nice to me and maybe I'll take you for myself instead of just letting you be sold off to the gladiator dens. Now give me a kiss." He leans his face closer to mine. I wait for the perfect moment and then I bite the shit out of his lip. I feel my teeth clamp together and a squish of muscle cut off. I try to swing my head back and forth, but his hand is still clamped down on my hair.

"You fucking bitch!" He punches me over and over until I let go. When I do and look up to see his face, I notice that his bottom lip is hanging off. Not completely severed, but only attached at one side. I laugh at the sight of it.

He puts his hand up to his mouth and groans in pain. "Mmmm, fucking cunt!" he barrels over to me and starts to kick and punch me. He kicks so hard the chair that I'm fastened to breaks and I'm able to roll into a ball once I get my arms free from the wood behind me, pulling them under my legs and back to the front of my body.

"I'll fucking kill you!" He continues to stomp and punch me, the blood from his lip dripping freely on me. I roll to the other side as one of the kicks forces me to cough up blood.

Right next to me is the broken wooden chair. My wrists are still bound, but I can move my hands.

"Ahh!" I yell and arch forward as he lands a hard kick on my back.

When I curl back forward, I grab for the wood right next to me. It's rotted slightly, but there are some pieces that are still in pretty good shape and they look to be sharp enough to do some damage.

I don't think it'll be enough to kill him, but it's at least enough to injure him. I pull the wood piece up and slam it into his thigh. I splinter my hands up, but the piece goes into his thigh like I had hoped it would.

"Oh God. What the fuck! Ilia! Rooster!" The man screams out and falls to the floor. I don't know what I did, but I do know that the second the man hit the floor and pulled the wood out of his leg, large spurts of blood arch up into the air. I lay there with my hands cuffed in front of my body and stare at him for a second until I realize what I'm seeing and what it means for me. I don't know the way out of here, but I have to at least try and get away. I have to try. I stand up on my feet and look around the space. The room itself seems like more of a storage room than a bedroom, but there are pieces of metal, pipes, and wood lying around. I pick up one of the pipes that would be easy enough for me to carry and hold completely in my hand, then I run to the door. When I open the door there is one of the security guards already on his way in my direction. Either he heard the man screaming or he's coming to take me back to the community room. I had to get rid of him.

"Hey, what the hell are you doing?" He rushes in my direction; I bring the pipe up and swing with all my might at his head. A loud crack erupts in the air and the man falls to the floor. I bring the pipe down over and over until he is no longer moving. I don't check to see if he is dead. I don't care if he is. All that I care about is that he is not chasing after me right now. I jump over his body and open another set of doors. There is a long hallway and then a set of stairs that leads up. I remember walking down this long hallway while I still had my blindfold on, but I don't remember ever being upstairs.

"What the fuck is going on here?" I hear people behind me, they are further away, but no one is in my line of sight yet. It seems as though most of the security guards are gone. It's eerily quiet. I run up the stairs. When I get to the landing, I realize that I'm in a home. It's not complete, in fact there's only the bones of the house up right now. Why the fuck would someone build all that space downstairs before they finished the actual house? This must have been a while in the making.

I don't really want to be walking around in an unfinished house, because I'm sure nothing is stable and also, I'm out in the open. There is no real place for me to hide. The second they come up the stairs they will see where I am.

I run despite the pain in my back and side, the pain in my arm, and the pain in my feet. I don't even stop to catch my breath. There are other houses further down that are either complete or semi-complete. I don't know where this place is located, but I don't think I'm able to run home. I need to come up with a plan, I need to think straight for a second.

I hear engines and people screaming, but I don't turn around to see how close or how far from me they are. I need to focus on getting out of here, that is all that matters right now.

There is one house that is mostly complete, but the windows aren't in. I slide through one of the windows and press myself as far as I can against one of the walls. I bring my hands to my face and cry. No tears come out, but the adrenaline of all that is going on right now is starting to take its toll on me. I can't get my hands to stop shaking and my ears are picking up on every single sound that I hear. Several cars drive by, but I don't look up to see where they are stopping. I don't want to risk it and be seen.

"She's here. I know that fucking bitch is still here somewhere. This is the fucking reason you can't be nice to these cunts! They play you for a fool."

Someone screams out.

"I leave you boys alone for a second and shit hits the fan? What is going on?" This time I know the voice, it's Camy, she must be coming back from wherever she'd gone.

"One of the girls escaped."

"Shit? Well, who is it? The De Luca or the Bianucci?"

"De Luca."

"Whatever, she's worthless, have fun with her boys. I need to go speak with Ilia about the other one. We have our payment." After a few seconds I hear an engine come to life and a car drive off.

"Go over there and check that house. She's hasn't been able to get off the property. The gates are still closed. She's still here trying to hide."

I put a hand to my mouth and do my best not to cry. I've been in this position before, hiding from a man that was trying to catch me. The last time it didn't end too well for me.

Footsteps move in a different direction, but I don't know where they are going or how many guards there are.

"What the fuck-" One of the men outside speaks up, but I don't hear anything after that.

I hear footsteps moving in my direction.

Oh God. They are going to find me. My heart tries to beat out of my chest. I'm so close to being free I can't get caught now.

I try to do the same thing I had done down in the basement. I get over to the wall and just as the man crawls in I swing with all my might. It lands hard against his head, but it's not enough to knock him out. I swing again, but the man reaches out and grabs the pipe before I can make contact. He wrenches it out of my hand, then slams me hard against the wall and presses a gun under my chin.

Oh God, no.

I squeeze my eyes shut and wait for the bullet that is going to end my life.

"Oh ... fuck ... Bella?"

I open my eyes again and the man in front of me is ripping the hood off his head and pulling the gun away from my chin.

My breath gets stuck in my throat as I throw my still tethered hands over his head and down onto his neck. I hold him close and sob huge tears of relief.

My white knight has arrived, Josip is here.

18

JF

Josip

"*Jebote* ... Oh my God. Bella. Oh God. I'm sorry. Fuck!" I press my lips to hers and she falls into me.

"Josip, you're here. I can't believe it." She kisses me again.

"What the fuck is this?" I pull her arms up from around my neck and see her wrists are still chained up. "We have to get you out of here. "

"No, don't worry about that we have to go back. There's still someone in there." She pulls away from me, but I don't let her go. Honestly, I don't know if I ever will let her go.

"Bella, I don't give a fuck about anybody else. We have to go now." I grab her wrists tighter and pull in the opposite direction.

"No, please we can't just leave her there, you don't understand. Please!" Those clear blue eyes bore into mine and though everything in me is telling me to just run out of here, I'll do just about anything to get that look out of her eyes.

"Who else is in there?"

"There's a man named Rooster in there, a woman named Camy, and another man I'm not sure of. There is a new man named Ilia, and another I'm sure I killed. I don't know how many guards are there, but much less than what it was before. It's the only reason I was able to get out of there."

Surprise sparks in my mind. That's not a common name, but there is no way that Ilia is here. Ilia Vavra was the first one affected by this shit, why the fuck would he be here? "Ilia ... Did they ever say a last name? What did he look like? "

"I don't remember it was hard to see, though it's the first time I've heard of him though. He's never been here before."

This could be the proof, if it truly is Ilia Vavra that is behind this shit then Marko needs to know. I'm at war with my need to get Bella the hell out of here and getting the proof I would need to rejoin my family.

"Bella, if we go back in that room, you will do everything that I say. If I tell you to turn back and run that is what you do. Do you understand?" I keep my gaze on hers waiting for her to give me an answer. I want to go home, but her safety comes first, fuck everything else. If I get back home and they want to kill me, so be it. As long as Bella is safe that is all that matters.

"I understand, I'm with you." She grabs hold of my hand the best that she can with the cuffs still on hers.

I walk out the back of the still in construction house and make my way to the house Bella told me she'd just escaped. I do my best not to go over too much uneven ground as she's having a hard time getting her eyes to focus.

She keeps telling me that she's okay, but I can see the limp and the way she clutches her side when she has to move faster than she'd like. My woman is hurting.

"Are you sure you're going to be able to make it? You don't look good." The last thing I need right now is for her to drop all because I'm trying to find out exactly what's going on here.

"I'm fine, I swear it. I just want to get out of here as soon as possible, we just have to get Christine first." She whispers to me.

We finally make it to the long hallway that Katarina had told me about and I can hear someone talking. A heavy European accent and a cocky attitude to his voice.

"I need her family if I'm going to take over the east coast. I already have the entire west. I think maybe we need to wait a bit longer for her family to pay the rest of the ransom." I press myself as close to the wall as I possibly can and make sure Bella does the same. I push open the door slightly and sure enough, Ilia fucking Vavra is there talking to Rooster, a woman I assume is this Camy person, and his head of security Butcher. Butcher's face was carved up by a rival family, leaving him with just one eye, one ear, and only partial ability to speak.

I don't know what the fuck is going on, but I know Marko and the rest of them will be glad to know that the snake in the grass is none other than Ilia Vavra himself.

I pull out my phone and snap a few pictures. I take some video as well, but I don't even have the time to send it off to anyone, a large blow to the back of my head forces me to drop the phone and protect myself.

"Oh shit! Josip," Bella cries out!

I dislodge the person behind me, pull my gun around and shoot two times. The guard drops to the floor in a heap.

"What the fuck!"

Rooster yells out and comes in the direction of the door full steam. I stand behind it and throw all my weight into the opening door so it hits him in the face when he pulls it open, the blow knocks him out cold.

"What the hell is this?" Camy yells out as she runs over to where Christine Bianucci is, trying to kneel behind the kidnapped woman's body for cover.

"Josip? I would have expected anyone else before I would have expected you." Ilia says as I point my gun at him.

"Surprise." I smirk and pull the trigger. The bullet hits him in the chest wide right and he falls against Butcher.

A loud whooshing sound comes from behind me. Rooster has lit one of the walls on fire and somehow slipped out the way that we came in. The entire place is nothing more than tinder and rotted wood. We're surrounded by flames before I can blink.

"Ahhh! Rooster! No, don't you fucking leave me!" Camy screams at the door from where she and Christine are. The flames have them both boxed in.

"Bella go!" I turn to yell at her and it's only then that I see her with the phone still in her hand, the little light on. She must have been using it to see in the dark.

"No! I'm not going to leave you!"

"For fuck's sake woman! Go!"

She shakes her head again and I know it's no use arguing with her.

Ilia and Butcher have slipped out another way. As far as I can tell there is no way out of here that Christine and Camy would be able to get to from where they are boxed in.

"*Jebote!*" I curse and dart through the flames, my sweater and pants singeing, but thankfully not catching on fire. I grab hold of the chair and break the wood legs allowing Christine the ability to stand up. I grab hold of Camy and even though I'm her enemy, the threat of burning alive is enough to have her clinging on to me for dear life. There is nothing that we can do besides push through.

"We're never going to make it." Christine says from my side.

"We just have to run. Go fast," I grit out. "One, two, three!" The three of us rush through the flames. I'm not as lucky as the first time. My sweater catches fire first and then Christine's shirt.

"Fuck! No!" Christine swings her arms around in complete panic.

"Stop," I yell at her! "Fucking stop." I tug my sweater off as quickly as possible before I tackle the panicking woman down to the ground. I put the fire out on her.

"You!" I growl at the woman cowering curled up on the floor. "Either you find us a way out of here or we all burn to death."

"That way." Even in this intense heat Camy's teeth are chattering in fear. I guess burning to death is not high on her list of ways to die.

I follow her directions and we go through a long corridor of rooms, in one room there is a bloated deceased woman lying in the center.

The fire hasn't made it this far yet, but I know it's only a matter of seconds.

"Bella, phone." She hands it to me without hesitation. I'm absolutely ecstatic to see that she has not stopped recording. I pass the phone over the body of the dead woman. Even though her face is in my direction I can't make out who she is.

The flames are now licking their way through this door and the smoke is becoming unbearable.

"We have to get out of here," I say. The four of us rush through the last door.

"Oh God," Bella yells out as she falls and trips over one of the dead bodies on the floor. There is a pile and she has stumbled right into them.

"What the fuck is this?" I turn to Camy, but she doesn't say a word.

"The guards. They were killing off the guards," Christine hisses out.

They don't want any witnesses to what they were doing. This made all the fucking sense in the world. No witnesses, no one to tell everyone else what the hell is going on.

A loud explosion goes off behind us and the girls all scream out. The entire flimsy structure is about to come down around us.

"Fuck this." Camy runs to the next door leaving the rest of us behind.

"Hey, wait a fucking minute! *Sranje*," I grab hold of Bella and follow Camy.

There is another set of stairs that lead up out of the basement at the other end of the unfinished house. I tackle Camy before she can make it any further away from us.

"Where the fuck do you think you are going? The only way you are getting away from us is if I put a fucking bullet in your head." I turn her around so the woman can see my face. Only instead of fear, I see a stupid smirk on her face.

"What do you think bringing me with you will do? They've already won. There is nothing that anyone can do."

"Yeah, maybe they got away, but they didn't think you were important enough to their plan to take with them. Expendable." I get off her and pull her up with me. She fights me every step, but she might be vital in finding out exactly what is going on.

We make it outside and the Maserati is gone. I have no idea if Rooster went with them or not. The only thing I know for certain is I need to get these girls out of here fast, the fire is spreading from structure to structure, lighting up the sky. I won't be able to explain this shit if the cops show up. Marko won't bail me out either.

We run as best we can to my rental car. I stuff Camy into the trunk, Christine in the back seat, and help Bella into the front. The flames are rising to the sky behind me with the end of my journey ahead of me.

I take the phone and the eleven minutes of video that Bella has managed to take and call Kaja. Time to let the family know that I'm coming home.

19

IF

Josip

Fly is good on his promise, the second I get to the air strip the plane is there and ready to go. All through the small town firetrucks race to the out of control fire that we had caused. I wonder what the news reports will say when they find all the bodies. I wonder if that particular detail will ever get a chance to make it to the news.

I have nothing to get the shackles off Christine and Bella, but neither of them complains.

Christine calls her father the second we make it in the air. I don't know what they are saying, because they are talking in Italian. Though from the smiles and tears coming from her face I'm sure she's happy to hear his voice.

I use a few of the zip ties that are on board to tie

Camy's hands together and put some tape over her mouth. Just like Christine the second she was on board she did nothing but fucking talk. Except it's nothing that I want to hear.

Bella, though, hasn't said much of anything.

"You ever going to talk to me?" I turn her face so it's looking in my direction.

"I can't believe you actually showed up. I didn't think that you would and I was ok with that. I can't believe that you came for me." Her voice is nothing more than a whisper.

"Did you think I was lying when I said that I loved you? Did you think that it was something I spew off to everyone?" I don't want to be mad, but what the fuck kind of man did she think I was to just let her be beaten and killed, and not come look for her.

"Oh Josip, I know that you love me. But I also know that this rescue would not have come with anyone's blessings. You found me, but what did it cost you?" Her eyes drop down and it may be the only time in the entirety of our relationship I have ever wanted to lay hands on this woman in a way she didn't like.

"Orabella, I don't care who blesses us or what the fuck it costs me. You're mine. Do you understand that? I'll blow up the gates of Hell if it means you'll be safe. All this hiding shit is over. All this I'm not worthy shit is over. All this two different families' shit is over. You. Are. Mine." I squeeze her chin hard enough for tears to spring to her eyes. When she nods her head yes, I let go.

I sit back in my seat and shut my eyes for a second. Christine and Bella have already eaten and drunk whatever they wanted on the plane. The both of them will need further medical treatment, but for right now, there is nothing more I can do for them. I've already called Kaja and told him to let Marko know that I'm on my way with some information. I told him to bring the De Lucas in as well if it were possible.

All that is left for me to do now is to find out exactly what Camy knows about what's going on. She may be the key to sway Marko.

"I think it's time you and I had a little talk." There are still a few hours until we make it back to Vegas. I rip the tape off her mouth and she groans in pain.

"I'm not telling you shit. Never. You better just fucking kill me."

Christine is the one to answer, "No, they won't kill you. I'll make fucking sure of it. I will make sure they keep you alive for years. I'll make sure they do to you the same shit that you and Rooster did to us. I'll make sure that every waking moment of your life you'll wish for something as sweet as fucking death. Tell him what the fuck he wants to know or that will be your future. I don't know anything about what family you are working with, but the Bianucci's are the wrong family to fuck with."

Camy's eyes go wide and I watch her gulp down nervously. Her eyes dart between me and Christine before they settle back on me.

"What do you want to know?"

I smile at her and pull out my phone. Luckily, these throw away phones are quite advanced. I still have a bit of space left on the phone to hold more data. I open up the video player and start recording.

"How long have you been working for Ilia Vavra?"

"A few months ago, I found Rooster in New Orleans after things went bad with another kidnapping scheme that he was doing with someone named Vale. I didn't know him. Rooster is everything that I've ever wanted and he knows what the fuck he wants in life."

"Yeah, not you." Bella says from where she is sitting by my side. I squeeze her leg softly. I don't want Camy to stop talking just to be catty.

"Shut the fuck up you dumb cunt. You don't know shit about Rooster. He has his eyes on the bigger prize."

"Yeah, the prize, you've said they've already won. What are you talking about?"

"Once everything had died down, Mr. Vavra found Rooster and they hatched this plan." She shrugs and looks away.

"What exactly is the plan?"

"The lot of you, fucking dumb. Can't you see," she rolls her eyes hard and bounces her leg up and down. Clearly agitated.

"Dumb it down for us."

"Ilia exploited everyone's fucking weakness. He even had his own daughters kidnapped, because he doesn't give a fuck what he has to do to win. All you high and mighty motherfuckers walk around here like you can't be beat and all it took was a few kidnappings to bring the entire organization to its knees. You think we're the only ones who see it? You think your clients and allies don't see it. I guarantee that by this time next month, there will be a new leader of all the families. Italian, Croatian, Spanish, Irish. Ilia Vavra will be the one you all are looking out for and Rooster will be right there by his side." She chuckles before she raises an eyebrow and glares at me.

I hate to admit it, but she's right. I can't speak for everyone, but Marko Juric is revered almost as much as a fucking god. People lay down their lives for him. They pay substantial fees just to be able to say the Juric family protects them. He's feared and praised just for being who he is.

Within a few weeks Ilia undid all that. Not only did Ilia cut us, but he let the whole world see it. You never fear a god that bleeds.

20

Josip

Even before I step foot in the Košnica I can almost feel the tension in the air.

"We don't have to go in there. What if they don't believe you? What if it's not enough for Marko to remove you from exile?" Bella has been crying ever since I told her that unless I got enough proof that Ilia is behind this, I would be executed for going against the Juric family.

"Josip, maybe she's right. I don't know about your people, but with mine, something like this is definitely a death sentence. Come back with me, my people will protect you. I owe you my life."

"No, I have to face this. This is my family and if they choose to end my life because I've wronged them then that is just what is going to happen. This is the life I belong in, and today may be the day I leave it." I think I have enough of a case to prove to Marko that it is indeed Ilia. I have all the information that I got from Finn and Doberman, the shaky but visible video from inside the home as well as the phone I'd picked up from one of the guards. All of it seems ironclad, but I have seen Marko kill on principal alone. No one would question him. I could bring him all this information and he could still put a fucking bullet in my head.

"There has to be another way."

"Bella, this is the only way. It's the right way. You know it and I know it." I kiss her forehead once and get out of the car. I take the tape off Camy's mouth as we have to walk through a populated public store before we get to the stairs that lead down to the Košnica. I drape a jacket over her wrist binds and make sure that she keeps quiet. She's petrified of me letting Christine take her back to New York. Whatever Rooster did to those girls down there must have been threat enough to keep her in check. She obviously is not strong enough to undergo the same treatment she dished out to those women.

The bar that we walk through has a few patrons. They glance at the girls' bruised and swollen faces, but no one says a word. There are a few gasps, but no one dares to stop me. I make my way to the door and Geoff one of the guards is there to stop me.

"Mr. Vlasic. *Hrabra si. Umrećeš večeras.*" He growls out as he stares down at me. He thinks it brave that I had even showed up, they must all know what I've done. He thinks today is the day I die, but I know for sure that he'll go first if he keeps talking to me like he's crazy. Exiled or not, I'm not going to let him disrespect me.

"*Pazi što govoriš.*" I warn him. If I come out of this alive, I have all the rights to walk back up here and break his fucking neck for talking to me like that.

He rolls his eyes, talks into his in-sleeve microphone announcing my presence and then lets me down the stairs. The three women follow me, Bella and Christine on either side of me, while I drag Camy behind me.

The second I make it to the ground level I'm flanked by three large guards who take all the weapons off me and escort the four of us into a large banquet room.

Marko Juric, Sven, Liam, Luka, Kaja, Leo De Luca, and another man I don't know all sit there waiting for me to come in.

"Josip, I'm so very happy you didn't make me search for you." Marko speaks as he takes a sip of a dark brown broth that is in front of him. "I'm assuming that by the group of women you have brought with you there is something you need to tell me. I hope it's good. Tell me something that's going to save your life." He takes another sip of his broth.

I see no reason to sugar coat it.

"The man that is responsible for stabbing you in the back is Ilia Vavra."

"*Nemoguće,*" Sven mutters out in disbelief.

Kaja smiles brightly, probably impressed with the information.

"Bullshit!" Leo leans forward in his chair, too, unbelieving.

Marko's bright gold eyes pop up to mine and he pushes his plate away, "Speak quickly." His face turns a deep shade of red and every muscle in his body clenches in anticipation of what I'm going to say.

If there is even a shred of doubt, he'll kill me just for suggesting Ilia had a hand in this. It's time for me to prove my case.

21

Josip

Quick. Thorough. Absolute.

The evidence that I provide to Marko leaves no doubt that it is indeed Ilia behind everything that had been going on. Camy with a bit of persuasion even explains the plan and how they were able to get all the women from their families. I show the records, call logs. The most damning evidence is the video. You can see Ilia and his known henchman, Butcher clearly on the screen. There is no denying it. There is no other explanation that can be had. Ilia Vavra has double crossed us. Hit us right where it hurt—our family.

"Josip, I should have known that I would be able to count on you. To hear that one of our allies has gone against us in this way is saddening to say the least, but at least I know that your loyalty is as strong as ever. It's time for you to come home."

Thank fuck.

Sven, Kaja, and Luka all stand ready to embrace me. If I ever doubted that they were my brothers the look of pure elation on their faces right now tells me I never have to again. The problem is this isn't over.

"Mr. Juric, I'm honored as always, that you would allow me back into your family, but I'm sorry to say nothing has changed."

"Josip!" Sven shakes his head 'no' probably thinking me a crazy fool to not just take the forgiveness his father is giving me and running.

"I'm not going to hide anymore. I've lost her once already; I will not do it again."

Marko drops his fork on the table and he glances over to Leo before turning back to me, "Josip, you embarrass me. That is not for me to decide. The rule has already been set now like before either you obey or you die. I don't understand why you would go through all of this only to put yourself back in the same position."

"She's my woman. Tell me would you fight any less for the woman you love?" I stand tall, there is nothing that he could say that is going to make me back down.

"Josip, it's ok. Please, don't do this." Bella whispers at my side.

I turn to stare at her, how quickly she forgets. "Remember what I said on the plane."

"I see I'm going to have to intervene here." Leo Deluca speaks, "Mr. Juric if I may? It seems this is my problem to solve."

"If you see fit." Marko sits back and let's Leo take the floor.

"It's a shame that Orabella's mother brought her into this life the way that she did. Forever marked with a seal of shame. Never to be more than just a ghost roaming the halls. Just as I would not want to be judged on my father's mistakes, it seems wrong to hold her responsible for her mother's. Several friends of the family have called to request you be released from your punishment." He turns to Marko, "Your son-in-law, Wire, I believe they call him, did the De Luca family a service when he found and got rid of a few loose ends." He turns back to me and Bella grabs my arm. "On the strength of that and the fact that you've returned with this information I'd be willing to give her over to Josip with certain requirements."

"What are they?" I ask immediately. She is going to be mine. I don't care what he wants me to do.

"Josip, easy." Sven put his hand up, a slight smirk on his face.

"They will be wed immediately, and the name De Luca wiped from her record. I don't want to be responsible for her any longer. Second, Orabella will never seek out any member of the De Luca family for assistance, from here on out she will be completely on her own. Lastly, neither Orabella nor Josip will ever try to assume any seat of power within the De Luca Family which would include any offspring." He stops talking and waits for me to answer.

I look at him then around the room.

Is he crazy? That's it? I would have done all that anyway!

I turn to walk over to the side of the room.

"Do you not agree?" Leo asks and I hear Sven and Luka gasp in surprise.

"Of course, I agree. I'm the bookkeeper, I need to make note of your demands. I want this in black and white." I grab some paper and a pen, to hand write all his requests.

He signs followed by Marko. I'm the last one to sign right after Orabella. From then on, she's mine.

A round of applause erupts through the room and I sweep Bella up into a kiss. Finally, I can do this and no one can say shit to me about it. She belongs to me now. I'll take her ass to one of these drive through chapels on the strip to make it official.

Orabella De Luca is a secret no more.

* * *

THE MAN that was in the banquet room that I didn't know about was a liaison from the Bianucci family, he is here to take Christine back.

Camy is taken by Luka. Where? I'm not sure, but I'm not positive she wouldn't have been better off with Christine. I've never visited the prison cells that Luka runs. For someone so carefree and happy, I often wonder how sadistic he could truly be to keep prisoners for years on end. I don't want to know what he has in store for the woman who put a hand on his sister.

Once I transfer all the information I could to both Sven and Luka, I am given back my belongings and allowed to bring my woman home. She had absolutely nothing, making her completely dependent on me. I love knowing that it's entirely up to me to take care of her and knowing that she trusts me enough to know that I will.

I have the family doctor come over to my home and look Bella over. She is severely malnourished, bruised, dehydrated, her shoulder is sprained, and she had to have over thirty stiches in various parts of her head. She wouldn't tell me exactly what had happened only that they pulled her hair really hard.

Besides that, she is given a clean bill of health.

The doctor sets up an IV of fluids to get her back some of her electrolytes as well as some antibiotics to fight off any possible infection she may have. I get her anything I can that might make her more comfortable.

It's taken me years to get to this point there is no way that I'm going to take it for granted.

"Josip, please! Just relax. I'm fine, sit down."

"How can I sit down? I know you're hurting and just don't want to say anything."

"I am, but you can't do anything about it right now. Sit with me. Honestly, I don't think I've ever had anyone fuss over me as much as you are right now." She chuckles and shifts slightly on the bed to get more comfortable.

"Bella, you deserve kingdoms to fuss over you, until that happens, you'll have to deal with me doing it." I lean down and kiss her forehead before I move towards the door to get more pillows for her.

"Josip."

"My Bella?" I reply to her.

"I love you."

"I love you too, more than my own life. Don't you ever forget it." I smile at my queen.

Finally, she's here and she's all mine.

EPILOGUE

Josip

Within two weeks I have my mark on her and a small wedding planned for Bella. She told me that she was more than happy to just go down to the courthouse and get a marriage license, but I wasn't having it. Bella has been denied everything her entire life. It's time she is given everything her heart desires.

Katarina demands that she be allowed to come. Apparently, they had formed quite the bond while they were both locked up in that hell hole.

Unfortunately, once Marko found out that Katarina had indeed given up vital information she was removed from her position in the family, all the years of her hard work erased in a matter of days. There is no way she will get it back either. Marko has deemed her unworthy.

The best she can hope for now is a good husband to be matched up with. It's a shame since she was very good at her job.

The rest of the family come out to support me as well. Sven and Luka shower the two of us with gifts and money. The women in the family make a fuss over her and the wedding dress.

They ooh and awe over the three carat ring I bought for Bella on short notice. Everyone does their damnedest to make sure that Bella feels as if she is part of the family. Once the ceremony is over, she truly is, both by the Juric family standards and in the eyes of the law. Orabella De Luca is now officially Orabella Vlasic and I couldn't be more fucking happy. There weren't as many people in attendance as I would have expected, because just like Camy had said some of our allies have suddenly found a better deal in what the Vavra family could offer them. Deals that had spanned years have been cut short, because they are now dealing with Ilia Vavra. He has a hand in every single one of our income lines and from what I've heard it's the same for a few other families as well. Quicker than we'd imagined Ilia Vavra had swooped in and took over. Marko Juric is no longer the powerhouse of the Croatian Mafia, we have fallen below the Vavra family. It's weighing heavy on everyone's mind, but right now all that I'm concerned with is Bella and making sure I keep a huge smile on her face.

"I hope you've had your fill of the reception, because I'm ready to peel you out of that dress." I lean close and whisper in her ear.

"Josip!" She turns a bright red and ducks her head into my shoulder.

"Don't turn away now, you're mine forever. You better get used to me wanting you all the time. We have a few years to make up for." I rub her back softly and feel her melt into my body.

The music is slow and calming as our guests eat the meal provided by the hotel. Instead of having the wedding at one of our homes, I'd decided to rent out one of the hotels on the strip for the venue. Now that I have all my assets back, I have more money than I know what to do with. I want to give her the fairytale wedding she never knew she had wanted. The hotel has done a great job at providing that for her.

I see Katarina standing by the side waiting for the okay to talk to Bella. I wave her over and after kissing my blushing bride for the millionth time today walk to where Kaja, Sven, and Luka are.

"They shouldn't be the ones to deal with it! He's our fucking problem." Sven growls.

"He was their problem first! Besides, it's too fucking late." Luka retorts.

"I don't know if they ..." Kaja starts to talk, but he stops when he realizes I'm right behind them.

"Josip, what are you doing away from that beautiful

wife of yours?" Sven asks, the mask he reserves for people he doesn't know planted on his face.

"She and Katarina are over there giggling and squealing about how perfect everything is. I don't think my testosterone can take the hit. What's going on?" I ask getting straight to the point.

"Nothing for you to worry about. This is your wedding." Luka smiles and pats my shoulder obviously not wanting to upset me.

"Bullshit." I shrug his hand off. "Something is wrong."

"Josip just leave it alone. There is nothing that you can do about it now."

"Kaja, tell me." I turn to the one person in the group that I technically out rank, if they wouldn't tell me as my brothers, I would make him tell me as his superior.

"Sranje." He sighs and looks around for a second, "Fine, but I don't want you running off to try and deal with this when you have a new wife to look after. You don't need to be the assassin anymore."

After hearing about the killing I did in order to get the information to Marko, a few of the guys started calling me the assassin. No one thought I had that killer in me. He's always been there just lurking beneath the surface; only needing a reason to come out. Getting my Bella back was that situation.

"I think I will decide if I need to do that." I squint my eyes and wait for him to tell me what the problem is.

"If you say so. I don't have the exact information, but from what I've gotten from Wire, Rooster has shown back up on the map. The Wings of Diablo and The Spawns of Chaos both are on his tail. Apparently, he's run out of places to go. It's only a matter of days until he is lying dead in the dirt somewhere."

Rooster's back.

Finally, the bastard that had hurt my woman is about to get what is coming to him. I have no doubt that the MCs will make sure he gets exactly what he deserves, but I'll make sure to stay close just in case there are some extra lessons he needs to be taught.

"Hmm, I knew Ilia wouldn't keep him around for long. Rooster was never the one we needed to be going after. It's Ilia. Ilia's head is the one we need to serve to Marko on a platter."

They all nod and a murderous look takes over all three of them. Ilia may have won the battle, but when going up against the Juric family, you would never win the war.

MORE FROM RAE B. LAKE

<u>Wings of Diablo MC</u>
Wire
Archer
Clean
Cherry
Prez
Ryder
Ink
Roth
Mack
Storm
Dillon
Pope
Treble

<u>Wings Of Diablo MC - New Orleans</u>

More from Rae B. Lake

<u>Jameson</u>
Yang
Bones

<u>Spawns of Chaos MC</u>
Shepard
Tex
Maino

<u>Juric Crime Family</u>
Sven's Mark
Josip's Secret
Kaja's Bet

<u>Eve's Fury MC</u>
Becoming Vexx
Free
Riot
Duchess
Sugar

<u>Dark Duet</u>
<u>His Darkest Needs</u>
<u>Her Darkest Gift</u>

<u>Boys of Djinn MC</u>
<u>Wyatt</u>
(Wyatt, Book 1 is in the Twisted Steel Anthology)

More from Rae B. Lake

Cody

The Shop Series Books
His Georgia Peach
To Protect and Serve Donut Holes
On The Edge of Ecstasy
His Peach Sparkle

Royal Bastards MC
Death & Paradise

Standalones
Drunk Love
Saving Valentine

FOLLOW RAE EVERYWHERE!

FACEBOOK
READER GROUP
TWITTER
INSTAGRAM
GOODREADS
AMAZON
WEBSITE
BOOKBUB
NEWSLETTER

NEXT UP IN THE JURIC CRIME FAMILY

Pre-order Kaja's Bet Here!

She betrayed me.

She should know better than to think I'll just let her make me look like a fool.

I'll hurt her, I'll make her cry but I'm never going to let her go.

By the end of it all, I'll make her wish she never took that bet.

Made in United States
Orlando, FL
10 November 2021